Falling Awake

RACHELLE VAUGHN

FALLING AWAKE

rachellevaughn.com

ISBN-13: 978-1539804383
ISBN-10: 1539804380

Also by Rachelle Vaughn

SUBMERSED
MAMA'S INK
HOCKEY GODS

Series

The Razors Ice Series
HOME ICE
FRESH ICE
WILD ICE
HOT ICE
BLIND ICE
ISLAND ICE

The Me Series
WATCH ME
JINGLE ME
TEASE ME
MENAGE A ME
SURPRISE ME
SOME OF ME: Me Series 1-5
PLEASE ME

Thorne Creek
UNDERNEATH IT ALL
RUNNIN' OUT OF ROAD

Dear Reader,

For years, Carli's story sat on my computer, patiently waiting for me to finish it. There was always a different book that begged to be worked on first, a new book to start, an old idea to flesh out... Now I'm happy to finally share *Falling Awake* with you, a sweet love story where the simple act of holding hands can give you a stomach full of butterflies.

This clean and wholesome story is somewhat of a departure for me. My other books have a much spicier heat level, but once in a while it's refreshing to revisit how innocent first love can be. I enjoy reading a variety of romance genres, so it only makes sense that I write in different genres—all under the same penname. After all, variety is the spice of romance!

I hope Carli's journey renews your faith in love and reminds you that hope, even when it seems out of reach, can save us when all seems lost.

Feel free to contact me through my website at rachellevaughn.com and make sure you're signed up for my newsletter. It's a great way to find out about giveaways, new releases and little tidbits I don't post anywhere else.

Happy reading!
Rachelle Vaughn

Chapter One

Ever notice how in movie funeral scenes there's always someone standing off to the side, looking ominous and mysterious? I wonder if there will be someone like that at my funeral. Or at Josh's. I bet Josh's family has everything planned for his funeral, right down to the hors d'oeuvres served at the wake. His mom probably already has her outfit planned and has already decided which designer shoes match her black designer dress. Would she wear one of those mesh veils over her face to look fashionable? Or would she wear her face bare for everyone to see her tears?

I had only ever been to two funerals in my life. Two too many, if you ask me. One was for my great-grandpa and the second, a year later, for my great-grandma. They were really old—both eighty-two—but that didn't make it any easier to lose them. I keep my memories of them tucked away inside my heart and I think about them whenever I need to be reminded of what it feels like to be loved unconditionally.

My grandpa wore thick glasses that seemed to distort the size of his eyes in a funny way, but he always asked me about school and let me sit on the arm of his recliner while he watched game shows on TV. My grandma had Alzheimer's near the end of her life, but I don't let myself dwell too much on the days when she couldn't remember my name anymore. I only want to remember the way she was patient with me when she was teaching me to cook and how she loved to do crossword puzzles on the front porch.

If loss is just a part of life, then why does it hurt so badly when we experience it? When people are taken away from us, a little piece of ourselves goes with them. Maybe we aren't meant to be whole. Maybe we're meant to be made up of pieces, some of them missing, some broken and irreplaceable.

I bet a funeral for someone under the age of seventeen—someone like Josh—would be extra tragic. All that wasted potential and all that time needlessly forfeited.

Sometimes I think about the oddest things while on my bike, pedaling west toward Josh's house. The ride from my house to his takes me about ten minutes and there isn't much else to think about besides the same scenery I've been riding past my entire life. Most of the streets were named after trees and I rode past Spruce, Pine and Oak.

Speculating about Josh's mom wasn't fair. I knew that. It wasn't like she was a bad person. She just had a lot of...*issues*. I'm sure most parents have issues behind closed doors. And most parents didn't have to worry that their kid was in a coma and when (or if) he was going to come out of it.

Unlike Josh's mom, I couldn't afford to think negatively. In Josh's case it was *when*, definitely not a question of *if* he was going to wake up. If Josh knew I had already given up on him, along with most everyone else, then he'd ostracize me for sure. He'd haunt me forever for doubting him. And if he didn't wake up, he'd have me to answer to. Either way you sliced it I was doomed.

It was summer in August Lake, June to be exact, and the town was already starting to feel touristy. That's what happens when you live in a lake town. Come summer, everyone from miles around flocks to the water and descends upon the town like a swarm of locusts. The locals simply faded into the background and took the tourists' money with a smile.

Josh and I wouldn't be going to the lake together this summer. In fact, Josh wouldn't be doing much of *anything* if he didn't get his act together soon. Out of the two of us, I was always the sane, reasonable one. And this little dirty trick he was indulging in had gotten old real fast. Comas were only supposed to last a few episodes on a TV show. Just long enough to work a few other plot lines in. They were *not* meant to last for months like Josh's.

It sounded strange referring to it as "Josh's Coma" like it belonged to him. Or like it had taken possession of him. Then again, I guess that's exactly what it had done. It had taken him from us and selfishly held him there inside its unconsciousness while it did who knows what to his brain.

After six weeks, it was beginning to feel like my coma too. When your best friend was lying in a hospital bed, it was pretty hard to resume life as usual. The fact that it was summertime made things even more unbearable. Then again, in September it wouldn't be easy to go to school without him either. No matter how you looked at it, "Josh's Coma" was a complete bummer.

I turned my bike toward Josh's driveway and glided down the steep pavement.

The Thornton's had it all. Wealth, successful careers, fancy cars, a custom lakefront home. But that didn't mean everything was easy for them. Josh was an enigma that no one had been able to solve. Not the doctors they'd brought in from around the country. Not the tests or the MRIs or expert medical opinions. No one could explain why Josh Thornton had slipped into a coma after the accident and had remained there for six excruciatingly long weeks.

The lush landscaping, the designer clothing, the piles of money in their bank account, none of it could help bring their son back to them. Josh was operating on his own timeline. And no one, not even me, could do a thing about it.

The luxurious house loomed in front of me, a bold reminder of all the things that had changed in the last couple of months. Josh's parents, Catherine and Warren, used to throw big, lavish parties here. They'd string lights on the deck and along the boat dock out back. They'd let Josh play his favorite music too loud, even if it wasn't to their taste. The house on

Lake Forest Road had been full of life. Josh had been the life of the party. The house was quiet now. Undecorated, unadorned, dark in the shadows of the tall pines surrounding it. Silent and still, it stood waiting for Josh to come to life again. Along with everyone else.

My house was nothing like Josh's six-thousand square-foot mansion. I lived on a quiet street on the other side of town where you can't see the lake from your backdoor. Most of the homes on my block were used as summer rentals and winter cabins. They were one and two bedroom chalets and nothing as luxurious as the Thornton Estate.

Four of my houses could have fit in the main level of Josh's house alone. His house boasted a family room, den, living room—as if one room to gather in to watch TV wasn't enough—and a modern kitchen that looked like something out of a cooking show. Five sprawling bedrooms sat upstairs, each with their own bathroom, each with a million-dollar view of Mt. August and Lake August. Outside, the deck had access to the lawn, beach and boat dock. Yep, the Thornton's had it all.

The Thornton's home had been decorated by a professional. My house hadn't been decorated per se, but was, well, *lived in*. My furniture had come from thrift shops and if I ever wanted anything new I had to scrimp and save all of my allowance to buy it myself. There were no free rides in the Thornley house. No rich relatives footing the bills for my every whim. No maids to clean up after my messes and no gardeners mowing my lawn for me once a week like clockwork.

Although Josh and I had our glaring differences, our relationship wasn't a rich boy/poor girl scenario. My dad made decent money as a truck driver and our house was fairly nice. It just didn't have a lake view and a gazillion extra rooms. And it didn't have a boat dock. Or stainless steel appliances, a gardener, a full-time housekeeper and a row of late-model cars in the four-car garage. Okay, so maybe we were not so similar in the financial scheme of things. But that kind of stuff was irrelevant to me. And to Josh.

My dad—along with our house—was super casual, and Josh's parents—and their lakefront house—were extremely businesslike and formal. Mrs. T wore mostly dresses and pantsuits with heels and Mr. T dressed in suits for work at the bank. My dad preferred worn jeans, NASCAR T-shirts, plaid flannels and sturdy boots.

Thankfully, Josh and my dad got along. Josh thought it was "cool"—his word, not mine—that my dad drove an eighteen-wheeler and made that horn-honking gesture that people, mostly kids, did on the freeway whenever he saw him. Josh never looked down at my dad because he had a blue-collar job and didn't work in an office. That was one of the things I liked best about my best friend. Josh didn't judge people based on their occupation. He judged them on their character.

Josh and I had been friends all throughout school. We had similar last names, and teachers being as unoriginal as they were, liked to arrange the seating charts in their classes in alphabetical order. Josh was Thornton and I was Thornley. Nobody ever came between us on that foolproof seating chart. Unless some Swahili kid transferred with the last name of Thornmeep, no one ever would.

In school, I wasn't popular like Josh was, but I liked to think he could be himself around me. Best of all, I think Josh respected my smarts. He didn't try to cheat off me and I admired him for that. Sometimes it took him longer to learn things, but when I related equations and problems to hockey, he picked them up quickly.

It was easy being Josh's best friend. He didn't treat me one way when we were around his friends and a different way when we were alone. He was nice to me no matter who happened to be around.

The hard part was keeping my feelings for him a secret. I didn't want to ruin what we had. If he didn't like me back, then everything would be awkward and we'd probably stop being friends all together because of it.

Josh wasn't the only boy I'd had a crush on throughout the years. In seventh grade, I had a thing for Beckett March. Probably because he smiled at me in Social Studies class and I interpreted that smile as a green light for romance. Turns out, he was smiling at Leslie Unger behind me and I felt like a total idiot for sitting there smiling at someone who didn't even know I existed.

After Beckett it was Joe Alonzo. Josh gave me a bad time for that one and never let me live it down. How was I supposed to know Joe only liked me for my math homework skills?

During freshman year, I had a crush on Marty Hanes. He was two years older than me and a football player. One of the girls in my gym glass took it upon herself (teenage girls are such matchmakers, aren't they?) to ask him if he liked me.

Marty's response? "I don't *do* freshman."

Sheesh, I didn't want him to *do* me. I just thought it would be nice to hold his hand in the hallway or kiss in his hatchback. What a jerk. I didn't need him to do me any favors anyway.

So, that was the extent of my high school dating life/romantic relationships. Not much of a portfolio.

Recently, I had come to the conclusion—or at least I had a hunch—that Josh's friend Mark Vasquez liked me. He always looked at me the way I wished Josh would look at me. You know, with that hooded eyelid, biting the lip kind of look. Mark always used my name when he talked to me, too. Like "Hi, Carli" or "How was math class, Carli?" instead of the standard "whassup" or "sup" like the rest of Josh's friends. They were too cool to use more than the minimum amount of syllables, but Mark always went the extra mile.

If I went out with Mark and Josh woke up I'd feel absolutely terrible. Like I couldn't wait for him to wake up so I was off canoodling with his best friend or something. I had no problem waiting.

Pushing aside thoughts of my failed social life, I propped my bike up against the side of the house and went around back to Josh's private entrance. Not many teenagers I knew had their own private entrance to their own wing of the house and it was a shame that Josh had to be asleep rather than enjoying the perks his charmed life came with.

Inside the mudroom, hockey gear hung from wooden pegs on the wall, and skis and snowboards were stacked against the bench. Josh's ice skates lay on the floor just waiting for him to slip his size elevens into them. It looked like he'd just tossed his stuff down a few minutes ago.

The room smelled like sweaty hockey gear. No matter how long he slept, the smell still lingered. And no matter how long Josh slept, I still experienced a flood of nostalgia every time I walked into his house.

Not in a hurry, I sat down on the bench and picked up one of the hockey sticks. Running my fingers over the frayed tape on the shaft of the stick, I thought about all the hockey games Josh had missed out on. How was he able to simply lie there in his bedroom while the Razors had fought for a spot in the playoffs? In the end, they hadn't made it, but Josh wasn't around to witness their effort or their history-making season.

I knew everything about Josh. His favorite sport was hockey, his favorite pro hockey team was the Red Valley Razors, of course, and his favorite player was Cody Lambert, the team's current captain.

Every year Josh dreaded hockey season coming to a close, but when it did he immersed himself in something else. Baseball, basketball, football... He was always busy doing something. Playing sports, talking about the stuff he wanted to do, always going and moving and planning. The only time he ever shut up was when he was concentrating on beating you at something because he was so competitive. Now he'd been quiet for much too long.

Sometimes I hear his voice in my sleep and the sound is so beautiful that I wake up with damp eyelashes. Other days, I can't remember the sound of his voice at all and I'm scared that parts of my memories of him are starting to fade away.

I miss the way he smiled so easily and never tried to hide it. He was terrible at playing card games like poker because he could never keep a straight face. Laughter would bubble up inside his chest, and no matter how hard he tried to press his lips together to keep it inside, the laughter would rip from him and light up his face in the process.

God, I missed his laugh.

Looking around the room full of his deserted gear, I wondered if Josh would ever be able to ski and snowboard again. Or play hockey. Hockey was his life. Would he ever wake up and be able to play again someday? Would he be able to recreate the smooth moves he'd pulled off last year, the plays that had made everyone jump to their feet, cheering for him in the stands?

Would he ever wake up *period*?

Looking up, I imagined Josh walking through the door, his cheeks flushed from the cold. He'd shrug out of his winter coat and shake the snow from his hair. He'd be raving about how great the fresh powder was on the slopes and ask me for the twentieth time if I'd seen the 360 he'd done on his snowboard.

In the springtime, he'd be tossing a baseball into his glove, describing the homerun he'd hit in the same voice as his favorite commentator. He'd readjust the baseball cap on his head and his green eyes would sparkle as he searched for lively adjectives to describe the sound of the ball cracking against his bat to add flair to the series of events.

Or, it was summer and he'd burst through the door, his nose and cheeks kissed by the sun because he refused to wear sunscreen. His brown hair, naturally lightened by his time in the sun, would have streaks of honey blonde running through it. He'd toss his Oakley sunglasses on the table and tell me how he'd managed to do a Backside 360 on his wakeboard. He'd ask me if I wanted to get some tacos and bring them down to the boat dock to eat while we dangled our feet over the water. Practically every day we used to sit on the boat dock and eat lunch. Did he feel a thrill like I did when our knees touched? Did he ever think about throwing caution to the wind and kissing me?

While we munched on our food, we'd make plans for the next day. Planning our summer itinerary was tough. We'd have to decide between going to the water park and going out on his dad's boat. Decisions. Decisions.

Now he was left with only one decision to make.

Shaking the nonsense from my head, I stood up, slung my backpack over my shoulder, took a deep breath and went inside.

When I walked into Josh's bedroom, Agatha, the day nurse, was making notes on his chart. She was middle-aged with threads of gray running through her mousy brown hair and she wore her typical uniform of scrubs and white tennis shoes. I wondered if the gray in her hair was a result of her stressful job or her age.

Josh's parents had hired two registered nurses for round-the-clock care of their son. Agatha and Mamie kept watch over him in shifts throughout the day. I didn't see Mamie very often because she was on the graveyard shift (a term I didn't appreciate), but she was nice enough to where I felt comfortable with her looking after Josh.

Besides monitoring his vitals, the RNs dutifully massaged Josh's limbs and moved him every few hours from side to side to avoid bedsores, atelectasis (which is just a fancy word for collapsed lung), and pneumonia. Right now, Josh was on his back, oblivious of the team of people who watched over him, dedicating their time to his survival.

Red Valley Medical Center, the nearest hospital, was twenty miles away. I wouldn't have been able to visit him every day if his parents had kept him there. Soon after the accident they were able to take him off life support when he began to breathe on his own. After a month in the coma, his parents moved him home from the hospital, hoping that being in familiar surroundings would help him wake up.

Dr. Patel, Josh's doctor, had an office nearby and was a friend of the family. He came by every other day to check on him and to make sure the nurses were doing everything they were supposed to be doing. Dr. Patel didn't know it, but I was keeping an eye on the nurses, too.

When she heard me come in, Agatha looked up and smiled at me. I smiled back.

Once, when I asked Agatha why she became a nurse, she told me about a nice nurse of her mother's who had given her a lollipop.

"Kids remember that kind of stuff," I had told her. Sometimes it was the most simplest of actions you remembered the most.

Agatha looked extra tired today, the same way I felt.

"How you doin' today, hon?" she asked, setting her clipboard down on the table.

"Good." I tossed my backpack on the window seat and joined her at the foot of Josh's bed. "How is he?"

"Fine. All of his vitals are good."

I nodded. It was the same answer she gave me every day.

Agatha stretched and rubbed at the small of her back. "If you don't mind, I'm going downstairs for some fresh coffee."

"Take your time."

Agatha and I had an understanding. She would leave and give me my privacy and I would let her know immediately if there was any change in Josh's condition.

Josh remained motionless in the bed. For someone who was fighting for his life, he sure was awfully quiet about it.

It was difficult seeing him dwindle away in a hospital bed like that. Every time I gave any thought to it, my heart felt like it was being ripped out of my chest. He was being fed intravenously. They were pumping nutrients into his veins, but it wasn't the same. He'd lost so much weight that he was just skin and bones now. Josh wasn't a big guy to begin with, so anything more than five pounds missing from his athletic frame was noticeable.

He had stabilized, was off the ventilator, and was breathing on his own. *He could breathe on his own*. If he could do that, then why couldn't he just wake up and open his eyes?

The rise and fall of his chest was deceiving. His body was allowing him to breathe, but his mind wouldn't allow him to wake up. Why couldn't he just wake up already and put an end to this dark chapter in our lives? We could swerve onto the road to recovery and exit this one-way highway running through Comaville. We could finally begin to salvage all that we had lost.

Even though I'd had plenty of time to research his condition, I was still short on answers. And rapidly becoming short on patience.

They say the body slips into a coma as a way to heal itself. As of today, Josh has had a month and a half to heal himself. That seemed like a long enough time to heal to me. Does the body reach a point where it can't heal or fix whatever is wrong and forgets to wake up or just let go altogether? The body is a pretty miraculous organism. Does it ever simply make a mistake?

I'd gone through scenarios in my head so many times. Where would I be when I finally got the news about Josh? Most likely I'd be right there by his side. But what if I wasn't? I could very well be at school or at home. Would Agatha text me "Josh is awake!" or would she call me breathless and excited?

I didn't think about the flipside of the coin. I could ride up on my bike to the red flashing lights of an ambulance. If I believed in anything it was positive energy. I didn't want the universe picking up anything negative and sending it my way.

Although the scans didn't show any brain damage, there was still a possibility Josh might suffer from it or even amnesia. Would Josh even know who he was when he woke up? Much less *me*? We'd be so excited to have him wake up and then he'd not know who the heck he was. That would be a cruel, cruel trick.

If amnesia were to happen, it wouldn't change anything. I was still going to visit him every day. I'd show him pictures of us together and tell him stories of things we'd done together and it would jar his memory. I hadn't almost lost him in the accident to lose him to amnesia. That wasn't going to happen.

Maybe he'd wake up madly in love with me. Who knew? Stranger things had happened and I was holding out for a miracle.

Tearing my gaze away from him, I looked around Josh's bedroom. So much had changed inside his room and he didn't see any of it.

The full-size bed had been replaced by a state-of-the-art hospital bed. Everything was white and sterile including Josh's hospital gown. Such a contrast to how things used to be. In the past, Josh hardly ever wore white. When he did wear a white T-shirt, it would start out that way when he put it on in the morning and by the end of the day it would be streaked with grass stains, smeared with blood from a scratched elbow, or powdered with dirt.

I missed the royal blue comforter that used to cover his bed. It was soft like a T-shirt and we used to lay on it while we did our math homework. His cherry wood end tables had been pushed off to the side to make room for high-tech monitoring equipment. And a chair had been brought in for visitors to sit on—not that he had many these days.

Some things in his room remained the same. Posters of hockey players he idolized and wanted to be like were still tacked to the walls. There were also posters of his favorite band, The Eggs, and a bright blue Lamborghini Aventador he dreamed of owning someday. The idea wasn't so farfetched if he actually became a pro hockey player. Those guys made big bucks and could buy any car they wanted.

An entire shelf of trophies lined one wall of the room. Over the years, Josh had earned an award in everything from pee-wee football to JV basketball. He was—or he had been— captain of our high school hockey team, the August Lake Lions. Ever since he'd been old enough to walk, he had played every sport under the sun—and some indoors, too—and had excelled in them. First place was always the goal. Second place was for losers. Anything besides first was for the people who hadn't worked hard enough or wanted it enough. That was Josh's theory about sports and life anyway.

Next to the dresser, a twenty-gallon hexagon aquarium bubbled soundlessly. Inside were three GloFish that Josh had named after Razors players. Ace, Hollywood and Cobra sucked at the blue gravel at the bottom of the tank, foraging for food. The second they saw me step in front of their colorful habitat, all three of them swam to the top, their wide open mouths begging for food. I sprinkled some fish flakes onto the surface of the water and left them to battle it out for their breakfast.

In the bookcase next to Josh's computer were a few binders stuffed full of hockey and baseball cards. He'd met a few Razors players and had their cards autographed. He didn't have Cody Lambert's signature yet. Even though he was the team's captain, Cody didn't make as many public appearances as the rest of the players on the team.

The rest of the bookcase was willed with some diecast racecars, a hockey figurine of Wayne Gretzky from when he played for the Oilers, and commemorative pucks and baseballs.

Josh used the adjacent sitting room as his entertainment headquarters. The comfy leather recliners and massive TV made it the perfect hangout and we spent hours playing video games and watching movies.

Josh's bedroom looked out over the lake. It was a view I didn't think I could ever grow tired of. Even if he didn't know he was home, his bedroom seemed like a much better place to be than a drab, depressing hospital room.

I'd sort of claimed the window seat as mine, but that wasn't any different than before the accident. After school, I used to sit there and Josh would twirl around in his desk chair and complain about his math homework. I'd tell him to quit being a wuss and he'd throw a pencil at me and I'd warn him against poking somebody's eye out.

As usual, the drapes covering the wall of windows on the west side of the room were closed. I went over and opened them to let some light in. His mom preferred them closed, but I thought some sunlight would do Josh good. If a plant couldn't grow in complete darkness, then how was he ever going to wake up in it?

In the distance, Mt. August stood guard over the blue lake surrounded by a red clay shore. The mountain was half bald in the summer because most of the snow had melted away. It was like a marbled white and green crown sitting atop the lake's edge.

As I turned away from the window, I caught my reflection in the mirror hanging above the dresser. I had Agatha's same dark shadows under my eyes, a consolation prize from insomnia. A worried expression tugged on my face, a consolation prize from caring too much about Josh. I wore my dark hair pulled back into a messy ponytail. It made me look younger and less of a threat to Mrs. Thornton. Or at least I thought it did. Besides, Josh couldn't see me anyway. If he was awake, I'd probably leave it down and make sure I brushed it until it was nice and soft and shiny. But he wasn't.

Unconcerned with my shabby appearance, I went around to the side of the bed. "Hi, Josh. It's me, Carli."

In the early days of Josh's coma, Dr. Patel told me that there was a possibility that Josh could hear it when I talked to him. Needless to say, I'd been talking to Josh ever since.

The chair beside the bed was fairly comfortable and I pulled up my knees and hugged them to my chest. "Hunter and Dakota and a bunch of other kids are going up to the Falls today. The sooner you wake up, the sooner you can do that kind of stuff again. Remember when we used to walk to the Falls, Josh?"

August Falls was a popular tourist attraction, but also a place the local kids liked to hang out at. There were hiking trails, a picnic area, a lake and a campground.

I tell myself that Josh being in a coma hasn't really affected anything this summer. What would I be doing on a normal June day anyway? Probably studying or reading.

No, that wasn't completely true. Josh probably would've dragged me down to the lake to fish off the end of the dock or talked me into going to a baseball game. Things *would* be different. We'd be laughing, enjoying the warm summer sun and making memories to look back on. We wouldn't be stuck inside his bedroom while life passed us by and while everyone else from school was having the time of their lives at the Falls.

I'd always wanted to go to the Falls alone with Josh. Just him and me. Not to hike or fish, but for Josh to kiss me on the observation deck. The scene was naturally set for romance, the perfect place for a first kiss. The waterfall would thunder and crash a few feet away, the mist cold and refreshing on our faces, and Josh would press his lips to mine in a fairytale moment. It was a silly thought and something that would never happen in a million years, but it was still fun to think about.

Last week, when I was feeling extra brave, I told Josh about my fantasy just to see if I could get a reaction from him. But it didn't work. He didn't even bat an eyelash.

The last time we'd gone to the Falls was with a group of Josh's friends. We browsed the gift shop and then hiked to the top of the waterfall. Once we got there, we threw rocks into the water. There was no kissing or holding hands.

Josh's friend Mark told everyone he saw a bear just so the girls would run away screaming, but I didn't fall for it. I think Josh liked that I wasn't like other girls in that way. I wasn't as squeamish as them and I liked to play video games, so I was okay in his book.

When I heard Josh took Kendall to the Falls (right before the accident), the twinge of jealousy that clenched my entire body took my breath away. When I tried to picture the two of them there, I couldn't. I could only ever see myself with him.

Yes, Josh had a girlfriend. Kendall Lamont. How infuriating was that? It might bother me a lot more, but I was rarely reminded of their relationship. Not that they had one anymore. For reasons unbeknownst to me, Kendall never once came to visit Josh after the accident.

While Agatha was downstairs taking a break, I told Josh about the book I was reading about coma patients. "You'd better snap out of it," I told him sternly. "Or, before you know it, you'll wake up and be thirty-five. I'd like to say I'd wait for you, but what if I meet some great guy at college and he sweeps me off my feet?"

I'd give Josh until graduation to wake up and then…well, I didn't know what would happen if he still didn't gain consciousness by then. I would go away to college. And it wouldn't be fair to hold me responsible for what happened when I got there.

"How would you feel if you woke up and I was married with a bunch of kids?" I asked Josh loudly enough so he could hear me through the haze. "I'd still visit you every day, though. My new husband would just have to accept that I knew you long before he came along."

This was how I spent my time with Josh now. Talking and talking. Maybe he would never wake up and I'd be left talking to myself for eternity.

Some days, the sound of my own voice was soothing and sometimes it grated on my nerves. I wanted to believe that he could actually hear me, I really did, but what if he couldn't? What if I was talking to him, rambling on about nothingness, and he couldn't even hear me through that deep sleep he was trapped inside of?

Would he remember me when he woke up? During the past few months I'd read all kinds of bizarre things about coma patients. I'd read about how people had woken up from a coma speaking with an accent. Or in a foreign language altogether. Would the first words that came out of Josh's mouth be in Russian? Would he sound like he was from Down Under and add the word *mate* to the end of his sentences?

Sometimes I played music that I liked and that Josh always made fun of, just to see if he'd wake up and tell me to "turn that junk off." It didn't work though. I also played music he liked, music we both hated, old music, new music... He never stirred as much as a sigh. As the weeks passed, he continued to lay there motionless and unfazed by my best attempts to rouse him from Dreamland.

I read comic books and hockey magazines to him, too. Once, I even brought lunch from In-N-Out—and shared it with Agatha, of course—hoping the smell of his favorite fast food hamburger would rouse him awake. I felt slightly guilty, but what if it worked? Besides, I was *hungry*. After that, I'd gotten into the habit of buying his favorite foods and waving them under his nose. Then I'd eat them and immediately feel bad about it.

Sometimes I threatened him. I'd tell him I was going to shave his head bald or paint his fingernails hot pink just to see if I'd get a reaction out of him. But that never worked either. Of course, I'd never do something like that to him. But you can't blame me for trying. Everyone else had long since run out of ideas, so it was up to me to keep making an effort.

My world was narrowing down into a succession of maybes. As in "maybe if I do *this*, Josh will wake up" and "maybe if I do *that*, this will finally be the day that Josh wakes up. "Maybe if I say *this* or think *that*, he'll finally shake himself out of the darkness and return to me." I guess it's easy to get caught up in superstition when someone you care about is unwell.

Some days I tried not to think about the past, before the accident, because it was too painful. And some days it was all I could talk about and the memories of our time together made me laugh when I told them to Josh. The memories sounded more like fictional stories to me now and not actual events that happened. If I was the only one to remember them, did that mean they hadn't really happened?

From age ten on, every memory I had Josh was in. When he woke up, would he remember all the things we'd done together? I desperately hoped so. He *couldn't* forget. I wouldn't let him. That's why I had to remind him and retell the stories so he wouldn't let them slip from his memory.

What if he forgot about *me*? Questions like these were intended to drive me insane. So, I kept them to a minimum. Or I tried to at least. Being rational in such surreal circumstances wasn't easy.

Each new day brought a different emotion swirling around in my brain. One day I'd be angry. Angry at the world, angry at Josh, angry that he was missing out on so much. It didn't matter that *I* was missing out on things. I was a bookworm who didn't do much anyway. But Josh, he was the athlete, the prankster, the jokester. Did he even know what he was missing out on? Or was he just oblivious to it all? Lying there in the heavy fog that held him in place each and every day.

I would have gladly given my life in place of his if it meant he didn't have to be in a coma anymore. I would be dead and he would be alive. Instead of how things were now. Now, we were both in a state of limbo, hovering between life and death. Waiting. Oh, the waiting was excruciating.

I was reminded of all those big words Mrs. Reed had tried to get us to use (and remember the meaning and spelling of) in sophomore English class. Obsequious, cacophony, vociferous, exponentially… It was exponentially difficult, this business of sitting around and waiting.

Other days I was depressed and alone. Honestly, the loneliness was starting to eat at me. Even though there were people around, it felt like I was completely forsaken. Sometimes I found myself on the verge of tears and I didn't even know why. It's not like I'd ever had a bunch of friends *before* the accident. But with Josh…*not here*, I was truly alone for the first time in my life.

Jeez. In that last sentence I was going to write that Josh is *gone*, but he isn't. Not physically anyway. I could touch his cheek and hold his hand, but the part of him that could touch me back and squeeze my fingers was far, far away.

Okay, back to feeling alone. I wasn't, really. Agatha talked to me every day and asked me questions about summer school. She seemed like she really cared, but maybe she was just being polite because I was here every day. No, I'm certain she was being genuine. It's me who has a warped view of reality.

Agatha isn't the only person around. Sometimes I talk to Catherine, Josh's mom, too. Usually our conversations merely involved me asking if she was all right, but we did talk once in a while. She probably just thinks of me as a connection to Josh. One of the last ones she has.

Today I was feeling more anxious than usual. Anxious to move on to the next chapter in our lives. Anxious to turn the page and start fresh. Anxious for today to be the day that Josh finally opened his eyes and looked at me.

With plenty of time to kill, I took out my journal and started to write. I wrote *everything* down in the journal.

The therapist they sent me to see after the accident (to help me cope with Josh's condition) suggested I keep a journal and write things down. Not even just my feelings, but anything else that was bothering me. It seemed like a good idea at the time, but now that I really think about it, it was pretty ridiculous. I mean, what *didn't* bother me at this point? Pretty much everything about what I've experienced this summer rubs me the wrong way. And why shouldn't it? In the span of two seconds I lost my best friend in the world and I don't know how to get him back.

By the way, I only lasted two sessions with the therapist because she was determined to prepare me for Josh's death and I wouldn't hear of it. Too much of a jinx. Besides, I couldn't prepare myself for Josh's death. I was too busy preparing myself for when he finally woke up.

So, out of boredom and curiosity, I kept a diary starting on Day One of Josh's coma. Some days I wrote a detailed account of the day and others I simply wrote down what the weather was like or what I had for breakfast. I didn't expect I'd fill up so many pages, but the days kept passing.

At first, it was just to keep track of what the doctor's said about Josh so I could look up their big words later on my computer at home. The hospital can be overwhelming, and it helped to write things down. I felt too stupid to ask the doctors and nurses to explain and they always seemed so busy and rushed that I didn't want to take up any more of their precious time with childish questions. So, I spent a lot of time at the library researching Josh's condition.

Then, as the weeks turned into months, I thought it might be nice to give to Josh a written account of everything, so he'd have some idea of what went on while he was asleep. If it were me, if I was the one who was unconscious for months on end, I would want to know what I had missed out on. It wasn't to rub it in that he was missing everything, it was so he'd have some way to account for the past couple months of his life.

Sometimes I wondered…If I didn't keep this journal, would I be able to keep the days straight? Without full days of school, the days seemed to roll into one. In summer, we never paid much attention to what day it was.

"Every day is Saturday in June," Josh would say.

What day is it today, where you are, Josh? Is it Saturday?

Day 42
The new house on the corner of Pine and Willow burned down last night. I heard the sirens after I went to bed and got back up again to ride my bike over to see what was going on. Fire trucks were lined up in

front of the house and all the neighbors were gathered around speculating about the cause.

The sound of the fire was louder than I thought it would be. I had to squint at how bright the flames were against the black night sky. Bright orange flames licked at the structure and all I could think about was the fact that their whole life was going up in flames.

I guess the family that lives there went out for ice cream and left a lamp on. One of their dogs didn't make it out. The more I think about it, the sadder I get.

My hand began to cramp up and I started to develop an indentation on the side of my middle finger from gripping the pen and pressing down too hard on the paper. I supposed it would have been a lot easier to keep a journal on a tablet or a laptop, but I don't have one. Couldn't afford one. I needed something portable like good old fashioned pen and paper because I never knew when the mood or opportunity to write would strike me.

If Josh saw me schlepping a journal around, he'd probably tease me about it. At first. Then he'd probably think it was neat that I had dedicated myself to something so completely. The same way he'd been with hockey and sports in general. He was the first one to show up to practice and the last one to leave. He did whatever it took to stay a step ahead of the rest of his teammates. That's how I knew he was going to snap out of his coma. Because Josh Thornton never backed down and he never gave up on something he believed in. And I believed in him the way he believed in hockey.

Josh's hoodie with the image of wings on a pair of ice skates hung on the back of his door. He once said that being on the ice felt like flying.

"Wake up, Josh," I pleaded. "*Please*. Don't you want to fly again?"

Chapter Two

Gordie, Josh's dog, trotted in from outside and I put my journal away so I could give him my undivided attention. Josh had named him after the Gordie Prince Cup, the championship trophy of the UNHL—the United National Hockey League. Josh had rescued Gordie from the county animal shelter four summers ago. I think Josh picked out the ugliest, scraggliest dog just to spite his mom. Catherine wanted to special order Josh a purebred something or other from the internet. He could've had a beautiful dog worth thousands and instead Josh had chosen a mutt with crooked teeth and mottled fur.

Gordie was awesome. He was smarter than some humans I knew and he had a great personality. Josh's mom still cringed whenever Gordie was around and Josh got a kick out of that. Josh knew you didn't have to pay thousands of dollars to find a good companion. A dog from the shelter was probably more appreciative of a good home anyway.

As for me, well, I didn't care what Gordie looked like. Josh loved him and that was good enough for me. Kendall didn't even like Gordie. Just because Gordie didn't have a shiny, glossy coat and a perfect pedigree didn't mean he didn't deserve to be loved.

I wasn't the only one who didn't understand why Josh wouldn't wake up. Gordie couldn't figure out why his best buddy hadn't moved from his bed in weeks.

I grabbed a dog treat from the box on the shelf. With Josh in a coma, caring for Gordie was left to me. Familiar with the drill, Gordie slammed his butt onto the floor and pawed the air with his front paw. I shook his paw and gave him his reward. He crunched loudly on the treat and quickly swallowed it in one gulp.

I scratched Gordie behind the ears and his tail thumped on the floor in response. His tongue lolled out of his mouth and rested between his teeth making him look a little crazy.

"He'll wake up soon, Gord," I said cheerfully. "Then we'll all take a hike to the Falls together."

The dog perked up and his tail wagged like it was on the back of a helicopter.

"You like that idea?"

Gordie whined and gave my hand a lick.

Careful not to jostle his IVs, I laced my fingers through Josh's and imagined us holding hands at school. Everyone would look at us and whisper that they'd suspected for years that something had been going on between us. I'd just smile and hold my head high because I was Josh Thornton's girlfriend.

But I wasn't Josh's girlfriend now.

So then what was I? *Who* was I? The only person who visited Josh? When none of his other friends would? That seemed like a lousy title. It implied that he wasn't important enough for people to make the effort to visit. And he *was* important.

I wanted him to wake up so he could answer all of my questions. I wanted to press my lips to his. His eyes would flutter open like Sleeping Beauty and we'd skip off into the forest together while birds sang about springtime. Just like in the fairytales my mom used to read to me. But fairytales were a long way from reality.

Before the accident we hardly ever touched. He took my hand to help me onto his parent's boat. We swatted playfully at each other. But never anything intimate. Nothing that friends wouldn't do.

It felt strange touching him now without him knowing. But what if he did know and it helped to jar him out of the coma?

My life was full of what ifs and some days it felt like I was drowning in them. Too bad Josh wasn't awake to throw me a life preserver.

I always wondered if Josh knew how I felt about him. I never gave him any clues—not deliberately anyway. I tried to be myself without fawning all over him like other girls. I would rather just be friends than for him to reject me and never get to be around him at all.

Once in a while, I caught him looking at me with a faraway look on his face and my heart would flutter and my mind would think that maybe he knew. Maybe his heart had finally caught up with mine. But it never did. I didn't blame him for being oblivious to my feelings. After all, I made sure to behave like one of the guys.

The day Josh and Kendall started going out, I knew he most likely didn't know how deep my feelings for him ran. Otherwise, he wouldn't have kissed her in front of me. He might as well have stabbed me in the heart with his skate blade. It hurt like crazy seeing him with another girl, but she *was* pretty and she seemed like the type of girl he belonged with anyway. Pretty and popular. Wasn't that always the way?

Thankfully, Josh didn't leave me in the dust once Kendall came into the picture. If anything, he spent as much time with me as ever. Which was a good thing.

Surprisingly enough, Josh talked to me about stuff he wouldn't dare say to his guy friends. Like how he liked the poem Mrs. Sandusky read in freshman English class. Most boys in her class were preoccupied by her DD's, so I was pleasantly surprised he'd paid attention to what was going on above her neck.

Or the time he confided in me about his plans for after high school. His parents were dead set on him earning a business degree and/or following in his father's footsteps and getting into finance, but Josh had his heart set on becoming a star hockey player. He never told that to anyone but me. He had confided in me about a lot of things. While Kendall served as his bobblehead arm candy, Josh chose me to share his hopes and dreams with.

With Gordie laying at my feet and Josh's hand in mine, I decided to sing Josh a song. I wasn't the best singer in the world, but maybe the melody would reach him. I could have sung one of the songs my mom had hummed to me when I was little or one written by my favorite band, Crush 21, but I had made up my own in my spare time.

I started to sing, my voice scratchy and tight.

I will wait for you…
Though the leaves on the trees change colors
And the birds sing a different tune
I will wait for you
Even when the clouds turn black or
When the sun shines bright
Or the sky is blue
I will wait

My voice cracked and the song I'd written for Josh died in my throat.

Contrary to what it looked like, Josh wasn't in some sort of stasis. He was still aging, his hair still growing, his fingernails still growing, his heart still beating inside his chest. His hair was getting longer and he was steadily losing weight. I wondered how long it would take for him to get back into shape to play hockey again.

I put my hand on his chest and moved it around until I could feel his heartbeat under my palm. It was strong and steady beneath the paper-thin hospital gown. But then again, the problem wasn't with his heart. The problem was buried somewhere deep in his mind.

I wondered what he'd think if he knew he smelled like a newborn. The nurses used baby shampoo to bathe him and I missed the way he used to smell. A mixture of his sport strength deodorant and cologne. He hadn't always worn cologne. The year we started high school, he received some for Christmas and had worn it ever since. I liked the smell of it. Georgio Blue was a designer fragrance and billboards advertising its manly scent were splashed all over town. Josh didn't bathe himself in it to the point where your eyes burned like some guys did. He wore just a hint of it. Just enough to drive me crazy.

A few weeks ago, I put a dab on his collar bone, thinking that maybe he'd smell a whiff of it in his sleep and wake up at the memory of it. It didn't work. Obviously.

Josh's mom walked into the room when I was smoothing Josh's hair from his face.

"His hair is sure getting long," I said, scrambling for something to say. I couldn't believe I had let her catch me *touching* her son.

Seemingly unaware, she pulled a chair over next to the bed and sat down.

Mrs. T didn't seem to mind that I came over every day. If she did, I think she knew I'd find a way to see him regardless. Josh's dad wasn't around much, but that was no surprise. He hadn't been around much *before* the accident either.

Gordie was a smart boy and knew not to bother Mrs. T. He rested his chin on his paws and settled in to listen to our conversation.

"His hair was long when he was a toddler," Catherine said softly. "I couldn't bring myself to cut it, but his father didn't want anyone confusing him for a girl. I saved the hair from his first haircut in his baby book." Her voice sounded far away, like she wasn't talking to me but to herself.

Today she wasn't slurring her words together, but I could still smell alcohol on her breath—from all the way across Josh's bed.

Catherine Thornton worked at some kind of non-profit organization. From what I'd heard, she spent most of her time at the country club "sipping" Mimosas. Judging by the way she appeared when she came home every day, I wouldn't be surprised if there were large amounts of guzzling involved.

It was a fact. Josh's mom drank too much. The designer clothes and glamorous jewelry from Tiffany couldn't hide her red puffy eyes. I didn't blame her or judge her. I simply kept her secret swept under the rug like everyone else. If I were Josh's mom, I would probably do the same thing to deal. Instead, I studied and read and tried to focus on the future. Had anyone in the world ever been saved at the bottom of a bottle?

Catherine cupped Josh's cheek for a moment and then stepped back. "I've never been a religious person," she admitted, "but I've been thinking a lot lately about God. I wonder if there is a higher being and if there is, how he can let these kinds of things happen to people."

I needed to believe there was an afterlife. How could someone have all these dreams and thoughts and feelings and when their body gave out they just *poof* vanished into nothingness? All those electrons and nerve endings? The human body was too wondrous of a thing to simply cease to exist.

I didn't say anything in return. I simply sat with Josh's miserable mom and let her be alone with her thoughts. The only sound in the room was the steady drone of the monitors. By the time she spoke again, I had already moved on from thinking about the powers that be to thinking about the class I had later that afternoon.

"His condition hasn't changed since we brought him home from the hospital," Catherine said hoarsely.

I knew that by "we" she meant her and her husband, but she could have just as easily meant me.

I turned away from the fear and cowardice in her eyes and inspected the ridges on my fingernails. "I saw his eyes move underneath his eyelids earlier. That has to mean something," I added, sounding hopeful.

Catherine's expression remained unchanged, as if I hadn't spoken at all.

Would she rather have a machine still breathing for him? Would that make more sense in her eyes?

"You're the only person who comes to see him," she said sadly. "None of his other friends have come by."

I already knew that. None of his friends had visited him. And his girlfriend didn't show her face around here either.

"It's too weird. He's just lying there." Their cruel words rang in my head, reminding me of why I'd always been so choosy when making friends with people my own age.

"They ask me about him all the time," I told Josh's mom now. It seemed important to her that his friends didn't forget about him.

That seemed to make her feel better and she rewarded me with a weak smile.

Josh's mom wore heavy makeup that contoured her cheekbones and eyelids. The cosmetics caked into her wrinkles, creasing her skin and making her look older than she was. Some women wore makeup to enhance their beauty. Mrs. Thornton wore it to hide something.

My mom had been naturally pretty. She never wore makeup—not that she needed to. She died of acute myeloid leukemia, a fast-growing cancer of the blood and bone marrow, when I was six. I was too young to remember her in the hospital. I couldn't even remember her being sick. The few memories I have of her are blotchy and faded.

I think Mrs. T drank because she was afraid that Josh would forget about her altogether and forget to wake up.

"I had Rita make up some lunch for you to take to class with you," she said briskly.

That was my cue to leave.

Desperate not to overstay my welcome—and be prohibited from seeing Josh altogether—I'd become skilled at recognizing Catherine's subtle and not so subtle cues as to when she wanted to be alone with her son.

This was one of those times.

Before going to class, I went in to use the bathroom adjoining Josh's bedroom. I opened up the medicine cabinet and carefully picked up Josh's bottle of cologne from the shelf inside. I lifted the bottle to my nose and inhaled. If Josh caught me smelling the contents of his medicine cabinet when he was awake, he would've swatted me away and continued primping in the mirror. He always took special care with his appearance, always kept his short hair trimmed and styled, even though it got tousled during all the activities he participated in.

I picked up his blue toothbrush, the bristles worn like he needed to replace it. Catherine hadn't changed anything in this room either. But why would she? It wasn't like he was really gone. He just wasn't completely here either. One day soon, he'd come into this very bathroom and brush his teeth with gusto and flash me a smile full of foamy bubbles in the process.

I picked up his toothpaste and held the cold tube in my hand. It was squeezed from the middle and I rested my fingers where Josh's had been not even two months before. I curled my fingers around the indentations and thought about how millions of people took for granted brushing their teeth every day. At home, I smoothed my toothpaste tube up from the bottom, careful not to miss any paste or leave any in the tube. Josh would squeeze a glob onto his toothbrush right from the middle, without thinking twice about the tube.

That was one of the biggest differences between us. Not how we brushed our teeth, but that he was carefree and I always thought everything through and analyzed it (probably too much).

The thing was, he hadn't behaved recklessly the day of the accident.

Summer school wasn't just for credit recovery. I was taking summer classes in a pre-college program at the Red Valley State University annex in August Lake. The seven-week session would enhance my college application and challenge me academically while earning college credit. Credit I could transfer to college in the future. Because I had outstanding academic records—yay me!—and demonstrated financial need—boo!—I was awarded a scholarship to assist tuition. Courses met for six weeks, with a final exam, paper, or project during the seventh week.

The extra schoolwork kept me busy and I was grateful for the distraction.

Getting a summer job was out of the question. The few hours a day I was in class and away from Josh were gruesome enough. Besides, my dad encouraged me to focus on school, and in the end I was grateful I didn't have a job to worry about on top of everything else.

Most kids my age couldn't stand the thought of going to school for four more years, but I liked the idea of going to college. And my dad was thrilled about me being the first in our family to attend college. I liked school enough to where I could see myself at college, collecting degrees and doctorates left and right until I accumulated every title under the sun. I knew I should probably narrow down my ambitions, but to be honest I wasn't completely sure what I wanted to be when I grew up. Unlike Josh, I didn't have a clear vision of what I wanted my future to be. Whatever I decided on would involve college and even more homework than I had now.

Maybe I could study to be a scientist so I could find a cure for cancer. Scientists had supposedly been working on a cure for hundreds of years with millions of dollars donated to the cause every year. How come no one had been able to find the formula? Maybe I should be a scientist. Maybe I could put the correct two and two together.

Until I figured out what I wanted to be, I was taking Women in Literature and Introductory Microeconomics every Monday through Friday for the next five weeks.

That evening, after class, I sat with Josh some more before it was time to head home. Sometimes I thought I saw him move ever so slightly, but I suppose it was just wishful thinking.

This time I wasn't seeing things. I looked down and actually saw his finger twitch.

I shot out of my chair and went to his side. "Where's Mrs. T?" I asked Agatha.

"I knocked on her bedroom door earlier, but there was no answer."

She was probably passed out.

How many times had Josh twitched and I missed it? Was this the first time? I just happened to glance away from my journal and there it was. A sign of life.

"It's nothing to get worked up about, child," Agatha said.

Why not? It was movement, wasn't it? Movement in a world where Josh lie dormant.

Confused by Agatha's lackluster response, I voiced the question out loud. "Why not?"

"You twitch when you're sleeping, too. I've seen you do it when you fall asleep on the window seat. I do it, too," Agatha continued. "Everybody does it. It's called a hypnagogic jerk and it's completely normal and very common. I'm sorry to say that unfortunately, hon, it isn't a sign that Josh is getting ready to wake up."

"Oh." She had burst my balloon of happiness, but I couldn't blame her for being honest with me.

She was right. Gordie twitched in his sleep all the time and it didn't mean anything significant. It merely meant that he was probably chasing a squirrel in his dreams.

Too bad that little twitch of Josh's finger wasn't a sign of what was to come.

On the way home from Josh's house, I stopped off at Gus Enterprises. The embellished name made the place sound like a lot more than it was. Gus ran an auto salvage junkyard and sold scrap metal and surplus equipment. People paid an admission fee, found the vehicle with the parts they needed and pulled the parts themselves. There were rows of wrecked and junk cars as far as the eye could see.

I rode past the front entrance and around to the side where there was a break in the fence. I leaned my bike against the fence and climbed through the opening in the chain link.

At my request, Gus had had the tow truck position Josh's car off to the side so that Josh could see it when he woke up. He would want to know what happened to his car. He'd want to see the wreckage he'd been pulled from—or more like cut out of.

There it was. Josh's black Camaro. It was just a gnarled piece of metal now. It didn't look like a sports car at all, but like some grisly art installation. Something that people dressed in black tie to see and milled around, nibbling fancy hors d'oeuvres and sipping bubbly champagne.

No. On second thought, the car was much too morbid to be gawked at and analyzed. No one wanted to ogle the cut marks from where the fire department had sawed him out. Or the smashed metal that would never hold its former shape again.

Upon closer inspection, I noticed that the left rear tire was missing. Had it rolled away that day? Did someone take it, carry it off to their backyard and string a rope through it to use as a swing? As I stood there and looked at what was left of Josh's life, was some kid swinging on his rear tire?

Josh's parents had given him the Camaro for his sixteenth birthday. Me, on the other hand, I wasn't in that big of a hurry to get my license. I should have rushed off to the DMV the second I turned sixteen, but I was dragging my feet about it. I guess I wasn't in that big a hurry to leave my adolescence behind me. Besides, I didn't have a car to practice in. Expecting a teenager to learn how to parallel park in a semi-truck was cruel and unusual punishment.

Josh was a good driver. He liked to drive fast and show off his driving skills and his 400-plus horsepower car, but he hadn't been driving fast that day. And the crash didn't happen at night when bad things are more likely to happen in the shadows. It was all in broad daylight. A guy in an SUV ran a light. As simple as that. Two seconds later, the guy would've hit the tail end and Josh's car would've just spun. Four seconds later—one one-thousand, two one-thousand, three one-thousand, four one-thousand—and the guy would have missed the Camaro altogether. They said the driver wasn't drunk, but in my opinion, you'd have to be drunk or suicidal to go through an intersection at fifty miles per hour.

Footsteps crunched on the gravel behind me, tearing my thoughts away from that fateful day. I preferred my visits to

Josh's car to be under the radar, but sometimes that was inevitable.

"Can I help ya?" a twangy voice asked from behind me.

I spun around and smiled at the old man walking up to me. "Hey, Gus."

Gus's weathered face softened and he sighed. "Oh, it's you, Carli."

Gus might look like he'd come straight from a cave in the hills, but he'd always been kind to me. No matter how many teeth he was missing. What teeth he did have were stained brown from his tobacco and coffee addiction. He had a mustache that would make Sam Elliott proud and a laugh that sounded like rusty hinges on an old Ford Mustang.

While Gus turned the other way to spit tobacco juice onto the gravel, I turned back to the car. Gus came up to stand next to me. We stood in silence for a moment and I couldn't help but notice that his nose had a whistle. I would have stifled a snicker at the sound if we weren't both staring at a tragedy. If Josh was here, he would have pointed it out without hesitation. Josh would have laughed all throughout the rest of the day because of that distracting nasal whistle.

I wasn't Josh.

Gus wiped his hand on his grease-stained overalls. "It's a wonder how anybody got out of there in one piece," he said, frowning at the car.

The cell phone that was hooked on his belt rang before I could begin to form a reply. Gus reached for the phone. Before he answered the call, he reminded me, "You know, Carli, you can use the front entrance."

"Okay," I said, my eyes never leaving the car.

"Hyellow," he bellowed into the phone. Gus waved to me and walked toward the shop, talking about parts for a muffler.

When I rode up to my house, there was a car parked in my driveway. Sadly, I recognized the car. And knew exactly who it belonged to.

Aunt Rhoda.

Great. Just great. My dad must have asked her to come by and keep an eye on me. Not that it was necessary. I guess her presence made my dad feel better and that was all that mattered.

My dad, who is rarely home, is a long-haul truck driver. He used to take mostly local runs, but last year we were hit with the humongous cost of repairing the transmission on his semi-truck and Dad had to take longer runs to make more cash. When our hot water heater and the washing machine bit the dust within the same week of each other, I knew I wouldn't be seeing much of him from then on.

I coasted up the walkway, hopped off my bike, and leaned it against the side of the house. After a few deep breaths, I opened the door and went inside. My house had two identical rooms with their own matching bathrooms on each end of the house. Sandwiched between them was the laundry room, kitchen, dining room, living room.

The first thing I noticed was the smell of dinner cooking. It was beef or something along those lines, which was frightening because Rhoda wasn't known for her cooking skills. The next thing I noticed were the track marks on the carpet from the vacuum cleaner and the straightened throw pillows on the couch. I wasn't a terrible housekeeper, but because it was usually just me around I didn't make a habit of busting out the vacuum more than once a week.

The washing machine was bumping around in the next room. I hoped Rhoda hadn't thrown my red shorts in with my white T-shirts. *That* would be a huge disaster.

I didn't really understand the point of Aunt Rhoda staying with me from time to time. It wasn't like I was ever home.

When I wasn't at school, I was at Josh's house. The only time I came home was to sleep. If given the choice, I'd probably sleep over at Josh's just to save myself some commute time.

Aunt Rhoda was the human equivalent of a turkey vulture, complete with beady eyes, a slightly hunched back, and a pointy beak-like nose. Technically, she was my dad's half-sister and that small technicality made all the difference in the world to me. She was nothing like my dad and that seemed to be just fine with her.

I don't really know why she took an interest in us. She acted like it was out of obligation more than anything else. Most likely she didn't have any friends of her own and my dad and I were the only ones around to fulfill her social needs. Not like she talked very much or was even remotely friendly.

I didn't know much about Aunt Rhoda—and preferred it that way. All I knew was that she lived in Red Valley—the city south of August Lake—drove a Honda Fit, worked at a supermarket near the mall, and was the least friendly person on the planet. She had an annoying way of speaking down to people and making you feel like you were eight-years-old and in the principal's office, answering to a crime you didn't commit.

When I crept into the dining room, she was setting the table. *Ah, man*, I groaned inwardly. Dinner with Rhoda wasn't on my Top 100 things I wanted to do tonight.

"What are you doing here?" I asked before she could start in with her usual criticism. And believe me, she would.

She glared at me like I had threatened her life or something. "I'm here to help," she answered vaguely.

Help? What could I possibly need help with? It wasn't like I had younger siblings who needed their diapers changed or acres of farmland to work and cultivate. On the contrary, I had a best friend in a coma and more homework than I could possibly finish by its deadline. How could Aunt Rhoda help with any of *that*?

"Oh." I did everything I could to keep my voice indifferent. I didn't mention anything about diapers or farmland because she was already looking at me like she was contemplating having me committed.

"I'll be in my room," I told her. "I have a test I need to study for." The lie came easy and I hated myself for it. But I hated her more for sticking her beak where it didn't belong.

She looked at me blankly.

Too bad Aunt Rhoda wasn't the here-let-me-give-you-a-big-hug-because-you-look-like-you-could-use-one type of relative because I could really have used one right about then. Instead, she stomped into the kitchen and stirred whatever concoction she was brewing on the stove. The she added something to the pot—probably eye of newt—and stirred some more.

Not one to stick around when the enemy invades your territory, I retreated to my room. Even though I had made my bed that morning, the comforter had been straightened to rival military standards and my pillows fluffed. I plopped down onto the bed with a sigh. She had been in my room. Fluffing and straightening—and *snooping*, no doubt—and there was absolutely nothing I could do about it now.

If she had been looking for drugs or paraphernalia, she must have been severely disappointed. I had resisted the obnoxious summons of peer pressure and hadn't even tried smoking a cigarette. Josh had shunned drugs because they would quote-unquote "interfere with his athletic prowess"—his words, not mine.

There was no reason for Rhoda to even step foot in my room, much less rifle through it, and her lack of respect annoyed me. Just because I wasn't old enough to vote yet didn't mean crabby relatives had the right to invade my privacy. My dad would hear about her faux pas the next time I spoke to him, that was for sure.

The few minutes of peace and quiet I had gained by retreating to my room were short-lived.

Rhoda planted herself in my open doorway, effectively blocking my only exit. "Where have you been all day?"

"I had class. Then I went to visit Josh." I could have lied about my whereabouts, but there was no reason to hide where I'd been. Everyone in August County knew where I spent the majority of my time.

"You're wasting your time," she declared.

Wasting my time?

I didn't know what to say. What about being friends with Josh was a waste of my time? What part about sticking by him and refusing to give up on him was a waste?

So, I said the first thing that came to mind. "Yes, this conversation is a complete waste of my time."

Rhoda's lip curled. "His parents should just have a funeral for him and get it over with."

Chills ran down my spine. That did it.

"He isn't dead!" I argued, feeling my face flush with anger.

"Not *yet* anyway," she retorted.

Had she just tossed words or darts at me? My heart couldn't tell the difference. There was so much ice covering her heart that I didn't understand how it could beat. What was keeping her alive? Hatred and motor oil? Because it sure wasn't blood and benevolence.

"Look," I let out a ragged sigh, reminding myself who I was dealing with, "as much as I'd love to chat, I have a lot of homework to do."

"I don't know why you're even bothering. You'll never end up more than a truck driver like your father."

I'd like to see *her* ace all of my classes. She probably wouldn't last five minutes in one of Professor Dodd's longwinded lectures. She'd get so confused that her head would turn to mush and she'd collapse right there in front of the entire class.

Wait. It wasn't like Rhoda had some high-ranking, high-paying job. She was a grocery clerk for Pete's sake! And yet here she was belittling my dad for being a truck driver. Some people really needed to have their heads examined.

I didn't know who died and made her the Queen of Mean, but I could really do without her hoity-toityness. I'm sure she was a teenager once—it is a prerequisite for becoming adult, after all—so I didn't appreciate her adding to the pile of things that were in turmoil in my young life at the present.

Before I could defend myself, she started in on my appearance. "You should take the time to brush your hair once in a while. You look like a homeless person."

There she went. Always criticizing me for one thing or another. How was that being helpful? Like she was so perfect herself.

That was my cue to shut the door—which I should have done in the first place. Two more seconds with her and I would have gone off the deep end.

I stood up and curled my fingers around the edge of the door. "If you'll excuse me, I need some privacy."

She stood glowering for a moment and I thought she might never leave. Finally she tossed her frizzy hair over her shoulder and flounced out of my room. I shut the door—slammed it, really—and put my desk chair under the knob for good measure. In hindsight, I probably should have sprinkled a line of salt across the doorway.

Later, I stood in my bedroom and stared at myself in the mirror above my dresser. I brushed my hair until it was soft and shiny. And then I purposely mussed it up and threw it into a bun on top of my head.

Chapter Three

Coma is the Latinized form of the Greek word *komo* meaning "deep sleep." Half of all coma patients die within a month. After four months, the chances of partial recovery is less than fifteen-percent and the chance of full recovery is low. One in ten patients regain their previous health—usually after months of intense rehabilitation and physical and mental therapy. The first year is the critical time for the recovery of consciousness. After a year, the window for improvement begins to close. Those are some fun facts I learned during this whole aggravating ordeal.

Here's another one: there is a fifty-percent death rate in coma patients.

But Josh was still here. And because of that, I put him in the fifty-percent to wake up category.

Maybe today would be that day.

To avoid an awkward breakfast with Rhoda the Dreadful, I got up at the crack of dawn and got ready for the day as quietly as humanly possible. After brushing my teeth, I slid on my favorite denim shorts. They were so worn and had been laundered so many times that they were as soft as my favorite tank top. Shorts, tank top, and flip-flops. My summer uniform.

I dressed in record time and slipped out of the house before Aunt Rhoda woke up from her beauty sleep. Lord knows she needed it. At the end of my street, Mr. Datozio was watering his petunias. He had the soggiest flower bed in the entire neighborhood. When he lifted his hand to wave at me, he accidently lifted the hand holding the hose and unintentionally sprayed his orange tabby cat. As I rode away, Mr. D was frantically chasing after the livid feline and the hose was left to soak the driveway.

The entire ride to Josh's, I grinned thinking about the horrified look on Mittens' face.

The sun filtered through the trees, causing golden light to glitter on the road and in the air like fairy dust. The trees hugged the road, almost as if they were discussing whether or not to make a run for it across the asphalt.

We didn't have smog in August Lake, California. However, whenever there was a fire in one of the nearby national forests, the sky became hazy with smoke, making it impossible to see the foothills.

Everything was alive around me. The tall pines reaching toward the cloudless sky, chipmunks scurrying across the road in search of seeds and nuts. And yet here I was, feeling dead inside. Or at least in a state of limbo alongside Josh.

Midway Market got its name because it was located midway between the town of August Lake and the lake. It was also conveniently located midway between my house and Josh's.

The owners of Midway know me—I'm in their store practically every other day. When I stopped in that morning to buy some more gum, my optimism was at an all-time low. The not-so-ideal time to run into a group of Josh's friends.

Josh was friends with everyone—or at least it seemed that way—but his two closest friends were Hunter Prescott and Mark Vasquez. Hunter and Mark were buying chips and soda, accompanied by a few girls from school.

Everyone was paired up—except me. Hunter was with Sierra, Dakota was with Mara, and Mark was with Julie. Mara was in a never-ending lip-lock with Dakota and I couldn't believe she actually came up for air long enough to say hello. Mark and Julie didn't look like they were together; they weren't even holding hands. But Julie stood possessively close to him with her elbow touching him in a silent *stay away* message.

They formed a semi-circle in front of me, making it look like we were about to do battle or something. The seven of us seemed to take up all the space in the small store and I suddenly became uncomfortable. I wanted nothing more than to get out of there and away from their watchful, scrutinizing eyes.

After the accident, I'd noticed that people looked at me differently. I never used to give much thought to what people thought of me before and I didn't much care about it now. But it bothered me more now that they had a reason to look at me with interest.

Sometimes I got the feeling that people felt sorry for me because of the way I visited Josh every day. But it wasn't me they should pity. It was Josh. They should feel sorry that he didn't get to watch the sun come up or watch it disappear behind the trees at night. Then again, I didn't want anyone feeling sorry for him *or* for me. We were doing just fine and when Josh finally woke up, we'd be doing even better than that.

To ease the sudden onset of anxiety, I pretended that Josh was standing beside me. He wouldn't care if the entire school had their beady eyes glued to him, so I wouldn't either.

Josh's friends were an attractive looking group. Most of them were on the hockey team at school, which meant they were tall and athletic. Hunter and Dakota weren't bad guys, but they did walk around looking like they had something to prove to everyone. Despite our differences, they were one of my only links to Josh. They cared about their friend and teammate, but they weren't about to sit around by his bed, waiting for him to wake up like me. Not when summer was underway and there were girls to impress and tans to improve upon.

The guys wore board shorts and flip-flops and white T-shirts because the sun would be extra hot on the water. If you wore black out on the lake, you were just asking to burst into flames under the harsh California sun. The girls had on short shorts and their bikini strings peeked out around the skimpy spaghetti straps on their tank tops.

They were all sporting golden tans, courtesy of their active summer. I, on the other hand, spent most of my time indoors, either in class or in Josh's room. Thanks to the olive-toned skin I'd inherited from my mother, I still blended in.

"Hey, Carli," Hunter greeted in a casually friendly tone. "We're headed out to the lake." He hooked his thumbs into the pockets of his shorts and tilted his head to the side. It was something I'd seen Josh do a million times and I had to gulp to keep my wits about me. "Wanna come with us?"

Sierra shot Hunter a you've-got-to-be-kidding-me look, but he didn't see it.

I could go to the lake with them and I might even have a good time, but it just wouldn't be the same hanging out with Josh's friends without him around.

"Thanks," I told Hunter, "but I have a class later."

Dakota wrinkled his nose. "You're crazy to actually *want* to go to school in the summer."

I shrugged. Going to class didn't seem like such a monumental waste of time to me. What did they know anyway? They didn't see the big picture the way I did.

"How is he?" Mark asked.

They all looked at me expectantly.

They always asked. Like I was their only lifeline to Josh. Or like there would be any change. He was either unconscious or awake. There wasn't any progress to report on. It's not like he'd be a little *less* comatose today than the last time they'd asked me.

Before I could answer, Kendall Lamont sauntered around the corner sucking on the straw of a Big Gulp. "Oh, hi Carli," she purred when she saw me. Her self-righteous tone was laced with superiority. She came to a halt next to Dakota and looked me up and down, her dainty nose held high in the air.

Josh's quasi girlfriend had a phony cheeriness about her. And that fake smile she plastered on her face turned to a scowl every time she saw me. Kendall always looked like she was sizing you up with a magnifying glass. Or attempting to set you on fire beneath one.

I didn't know what Josh saw in a girl who was so insincere. All I knew was that he had liked her and had taken her to more than one school dance. I could understand if Josh went for a girl like Anaya Rajan—she was super smart and naturally pretty—or even Becca Perez—she had an awesome sense of humor and her dad worked for the Razors organization. But the reasons Josh had for being drawn to Kendall Lamont were beyond me. Was it a status thing? Because that was so unlike him to place status above genuine feeling. Maybe he had simply wanted to be with someone completely the opposite of me.

"How's Josh?" Kendall asked, sounding only half interested.

I wanted to tell her to go visit him if she cared so much, but I didn't. "He's fine," I answered, giving her one of Agatha's patented answers. "His vitals are good."

Kendall scrunched her face up in a way that I think she thought was cute, but it just made her look like she smelled something rotten.

What did Josh ever see in a girl like this? Maybe he'd wake up soon and explain the big mystery to me.

"Isn't it *creepy* seeing him like that?" Kendall asked, her face still looking like she was sucking on a lemon instead of thirty-two ounces of diet soda.

Creepy? Josh was never creepy to be around when he was conscious. It didn't matter that he wasn't awake. He was still Josh. And what if he knew I was there? What if he knew I would be there waiting for him when he finally did decide to wake up?

"No," I said sternly. "Josh is not creepy."

"Yeah," Mark added, defending my answer. "Josh was never creepy *before*. Why would he be *now*?"

"Because," Sierra snorted, "now he's a vegetable."

For a split second, I wished my dad had forgotten to teach me manners because then I could snatch Kendall's soda out of her perfectly manicured hand and dump it over Sierra's over-processed head.

At least Julie had the decency to look as horrified as I felt. "He's not a *vegetable*," she argued diplomatically. "He's just unconscious."

Kendall shook her head and rolled her eyes. "*Whatever*," she mumbled around her straw.

"She *likes* hanging around him." This from Dakota, the guy who always felt the need to one-up everything Josh did. Dakota was probably relieved his competition was temporarily out of commission.

"Better her than us," Sierra murmured.

A customer came into the store, sidled around the group, and made a beeline for the beer case.

Sierra tugged on Hunter's arm and he gave her a what's-the-rush look. "All right, well, we'd better get going," he said to the relief of everyone in the store, including me.

"It was nice seeing you, Carli," Mark said as everyone turned toward the exit.

I smiled and watched as they shoved their designer sunglasses onto their faces and filed outside into the glaring sun.

After they left, it took me a few minutes to calm myself down.

Creepy.

How dare she say that about Josh!

I stared at the gum display, pretending I was trying to decide between winterfresh and spearmint. Gum flavors were the last thing on my mind. I couldn't believe how insensitive Kendall had been. She was supposed to be Josh's girlfriend for goodness sake. Or at least she had been at the time of the accident. Now she was just some insensitive, stuck up, infuriating girl who had tossed him like last year's lip gloss.

As I left the minimart and climbed onto my bike, I secretly wished her soda rotted out all of her over-bleached teeth.

You really discover who your friends are when something like this happens. I didn't have many friends before the accident and now I have even less. Enough to count on one hand anyway.

Using one of my dad's favorite sayings, I had put all my eggs in one basket. Apparently all those years of growing my friendship with Josh, I had alienated everyone else and set myself up for a severely lonely senior year. When I should have been out making friends and meeting new people, I was hanging out with Josh, playing video games, having swim races near the dock, and indulging in shoot-'em-up movie marathons. Now I was left to relive those memories in my head and hope for better days to come.

Even if I would be better off with some female friends, I don't think I'd be any happier, or any more fulfilled. I've always gotten along better with boys and never understood (or wanted to be a part of) girls' drama. Everything seemed to be the end of the world when it came to girls and their way of thinking. I didn't regret one moment I had spent with Josh.

Although, in hindsight, I could have sprinkled my friendship around to avoid such complete and utter loneliness now. Even though I still had a year left at ALHS, I'd already established myself as "that weird girl who still hangs around Josh even though he's not even awake." No teenager could ever overcome such a label.

So, I was left to fend for myself and hope the experience strengthened my character.

It might be incredibly selfish of me, but I was really hoping that Josh would wake up in time for my birthday in August. Or at least his birthday in January. As I rode the rest of the way to Josh's house, I thought about all the other important dates he'd miss out if he didn't wake up soon. The Fourth of July was right around the corner.

In Josh's current state, the holidays would be hard—obviously. But they'd be extra difficult because Josh loved them so much. Any excuse to dress up or celebrate or eat too much or throw a party and Josh was the first one there.

On New Year's Eve he wore those numbered glasses and a plastic top hat. He dressed in green from head to toe on St. Patty's Day. To take things up a notch, he'd put a drop of unappetizing green food coloring in everything we ate that day. He knew I could never get as amped up about the holidays as he did, but I went along with him to make him happy.

I missed his enthusiasm. He'd get all excited over the littlest things and not just specific days on the calendar either. Like when Dakota got a new video game, or a movie featuring his favorite actress, Lexi Laprise, was released. Every day was a holiday for Josh. That child-like wonder and excitement didn't whither up and die like it did for most kids past the age of twelve. It remained coiled around every cell in his body just waiting to spring out whenever there was an occasion for it.

"Mark got a new hockey stick!" he'd exclaim, nearly bursting out of his own skin.

Or it was something like: "Next week is Easter. We have to leave some eggs around the yard to rot and find next year!"

Everything was a monumental event. Like when Hunter got a new 10-speed, Josh insisted we have a bike parade and circle the neighborhood wearing funny hats and waving to "bystanders" that ended up just being Mrs. Marcel on her front porch wondering "what in tarnation" we were doing.

Or when his favorite Razors player, Cody Lambert, scored a hat trick. Josh declared Wednesdays Hat Trick Day and forced everyone to eat three of everything and insisted on doing everything in threes for fear of jinxing the team's further success on the ice.

You might feel ridiculous at first for joining in, but it would be impossible to sit out when his love for life was so contagious.

It all seemed so silly then, but now I'd give anything to have him burst through the door and announce that he just bought a new copy of the latest video game. We'd stay up all night and play and when I'd tell him I should be getting home, he'd demand another rematch.

More than anything, I wanted Josh to demand a rematch with life.

The holidays wouldn't be the same without his funny costumes and clichéd sayings. Sure, they wouldn't be the same without him anyway, but he always had a way of making every day memorable. Now the only memories I had of each day were of what I wrote down in my journal. When I looked back on my own memories and tried to remember every detail, I wondered how many little things had slipped through the cracks and were forgotten forever.

The idea of Christmas arriving in six months was especially rough because I didn't know if I was supposed to buy Josh a gift or not. I had to, because what if he woke up on Christmas Eve to find that no one had bought him any presents? But what if I did get him something and he didn't wake up until next summer? How special would it be to hand him a red and green wrapped gift in July? Or worse, what if he woke up when he was thirty-five? He'd wake up to a bunch of old Christmas presents meant for a seventeen year old.

Either way, it was an awful situation and I hated him for putting me in such a position.

Josh always bought silly gifts and never took anything too seriously. That's why I was having such a hard time figuring out why he was taking this coma thing so seriously. In all reality, he should have simply shrugged off the injuries like he always did and gone about living his life. Nothing ever fazed him for so long, so why had the accident? It didn't make any sense.

I guess that's why I sat at his bedside every day. So I could talk some sense into him and remind him that he needed to stop being ridiculous and shake this whole thing off.

Day 43

They're already rebuilding the house on the corner. They tore down the old one. It was weird to see the little postage stamp that was the foundation and the fence and bushes all around it.

Things can be rebuilt, Josh. No matter how broken they can appear to be, they can always be put back together again.

Even the most ordinary days can turn extraordinary in the blink of an eye.

I was sitting next to Josh, telling him about running into his friends and suddenly his eyelids fluttered. And then they opened and closed again.

He blinked. It was as if the world started spinning again after being stuck on pause. Josh had blinked.

He had blinked!

I yelled for Agatha and she bustled into the room a few seconds later.

"He blinked!" I exclaimed, my voice shrieking with excitement. And hope. Hope had been floating all around me for two months and now I grabbed onto it with both hands.

"He blinked, Agatha! What does that mean?" I looked to her for answers as she checked each machine and made a note of his vitals.

All vitals are good.

"It might have just been a reflex," she said.

Just a reflex? I'd watched him for hours every day for the past few months and I'd never seen him blink. It couldn't be just a fluke. This was real. This was happening. He blinked.

Day 43
Part 2

Today you blinked. It was the happiest I've been in...well, I don't know how long.

It happened really fast and I almost thought I imagined it, but Agatha told me she'd seen you blink once before. When I asked her why she hadn't told me about it—that's pertinent information, don't you think?—

she said that she didn't want to get my hopes up when it was simply a reflex and not a sign that you were about to wake up.

After I got home, I thought about how ridiculous I must have appeared to get so excited over the tiniest thing. Especially when you've done much more exciting—and difficult—things in your life. Like the time you made that spin-o-rama goal on the best goalie in the school district. Or when you did a backflip on your water skis.

But, considering the circumstances, that single blink I witnessed today meant a whole heck of a lot to me.

Next time you blink, I hope you keep your eyes open long enough to look at me and smile.

A girl can only hope.

Just as the world started spinning again, it gradually slowed back down until things were as before. After two days of waiting for another sign, I was forced to believe that one flicker of hope was indeed just a hoax.

I almost wished I hadn't been there to witness him blink, to see it, that little flash of life. Somehow it was like a cruel joke, the universe waggling its fingers behind its ears and chanting *neener neener ha ha*. If the universe was trying to tell me something or give me a sign, then I would do everything I could to get it to speak again.

It's oh so easy to make something out of nothing and read more into things than necessary. For example, the day Josh blinked, it was on a Tuesday. What was so special about Tuesdays to cause him to pick *that* specific day to blink? The time was 9:42. Was there some significance to 9:42? Of course, there wasn't, but for a while, I sure wanted to think so.

The morning of the day he blinked, I had eaten Cocoa Krispies for breakfast and rode down the street without holding onto the handlebars. So, for the next few days, I ate the same thing for breakfast and rode to his house the exact same way, as if those small details might cause the stars to align the identical way they had in order for Josh to blink.

Unfortunately, I soon learned that it didn't matter what I ate or how I brushed my teeth or what song I listened to before bed. Josh didn't give me any more signs of life.

Day 45

Remember that time we tried to make s'mores in your fire pit on the deck and Gordie kept stealing the marshmallows? Right now it feels like the coma keeps trying to steal you away from me. Every so often you'll twitch or blink and I think to myself, this is it. And then a day or two goes by and nothing.

Once, just once, I'd like it if you could look at me when you open your eyes and not through me like I'm not even there.

Are you in there, Josh? Will there be anything left to salvage of your memories when you do finally wake up?

The possibility loomed over us like a dark cloud as I wrote the words.

Do you lose a little piece of yourself with every day that you're asleep? Because that's what it feels like is happening to me. With each day that passes, I feel a little more empty inside...

Mamie, the RN who watched Josh at night talked incessantly about her grandkids. She went on and on about them as if she was the only person in the world to be blessed with them.

My mom's parents and grandparents have all passed on and my dad's family—all except Aunt Rhoda—live faraway in Tennessee, so I didn't know what it was like to have someone old going on and on about me. My dad's parents are divorced, but we usually got a Christmas card from each of them in the middle of December. They never sent me anything for my birthday, but to be fair, I never sent them anything on their birthdays either. My dad says he's not real close with his family (obviously), but Mamie acts like hers hung the moon.

I find that I'm entirely content with my family's arrangement and am relieved I don't have an Aunt Mamie out there shoving pictures of me underneath strangers' noses. Aunt Rhoda is in no danger of embarrassing me in such a way, I'm sure of it. I guess it's her one redeeming quality.

Here I am, letting my mind wander, thinking about family, and Mamie is expectantly looking at me like she just asked me a question. "I'm sorry, what were you saying?"

Mamie smiled. "I asked if you like baklava. I'm making a big batch tomorrow and would like to bring you some."

"I've never had it before." I crossed my fingers behind my back. *Please tell me it doesn't have grasshoppers or something gross in it.*

Chapter Four

August Lake was Fourth of July central. Everyone migrated to its rocky shores to barbeque, swim and scare off the local wildlife. Every year the city set off fireworks over the lake. And every year Josh schemed up some new way to celebrate.

Last year, Josh had arranged a full day of activities. There were raft races, a hot dog eating contest and water balloon fights. This year, Josh slept in the bed behind me, indulging in a party for one.

From Josh's window I could see boats zooming across the water, pulling delighted skiers behind them. Just when I was about to turn away, a boat pulled up to the Thornton's dock. When I pressed my nose against the glass in an attempt to see the passengers more clearly, I noticed that several of them were waving at me. It didn't take long for my brain to register who they were.

Josh's friends.

I waved back, making an effort to look enthusiastic, but I got the feeling they weren't going to leave until I went down and said hi to them.

The minute I stepped out from the air conditioned house, a blast of hot air greeted me outside. Reluctantly, I went down to the boat dock to see what Josh's friends wanted.

"Hey guys," I greeted, trying to put a cheerful spin on my voice.

"Carli!" Mark seemed especially happy to see me. "We're heading out to The Cove to watch the fireworks. Come with us."

"Yeah, Carli, you should come," Hunter added.

I glanced at Kendall and she was pretending to read the label on her bottled water.

"Thanks," I said, "but I've got Economics homework."

"Come on, Carli," Mark pleaded. "It's the Fourth."

"Thanks, but you guys have fun."

"We're better without her anyway," Dakota put in. "She'll probably get seasick and puke all over the place."

I ignored him and asked Mark, "Your dad let you take out his boat?" The MasterCraft was probably worth more than my dad's rig.

Mark shrugged. "He got a new one last week and doesn't care if we take the old one out and bang around in it."

"Oh," I said, like it was customary for every family to have at least two types of watercraft to their name.

It didn't feel right to celebrate Independence Day when Josh had the least amount of independence of anyone I knew. Even old people at the rest home got to veg out in front of the TV. Josh was locked inside his own mind, trapped in a silent, motionless world.

So, instead of climbing into Mark's hand-me-down boat, I waved goodbye to Josh's friends and walked back up to the house to spend the star-spangled holiday with my best friend.

The day was meant for celebration, but I sat in Josh's room and felt sorry for myself instead. There would be plenty to celebrate if Josh would hurry up and wake up. Maybe I should threaten to light a bottle rocket beneath his bed to get a rise out of him.

During the half-hour fireworks display—the county really outdid themselves this year—I watched from the window seat and provided Josh with all the appropriate *ooh*'s and *aah*'s, describing the pops of color in the sky for him as if he were a blind spectator.

Agatha watched from out on the deck and Josh's parents weren't anywhere to be found. I wondered if they avoided him because it was too painful to be around him or because they'd already let go of him inside their hardened hearts.

Day 50
Fourth of July came and went...

I had prepared myself to write about the fireworks and how Gordie hid in the bathroom, terrified of the loud bangs and pops coming from outside, but I couldn't bring myself to write the words. For so long I had put on a brave, cheery face in my journal, and frankly, I wasn't sure how much longer I could continue doing it.

How much longer could I hold out for a miracle?

Any other time I would have been thrilled for the weekend to arrive. But two days without school seemed like an excruciatingly long time.

The heat was relentless and all I wanted to do was jump into the lake and stay there with my head bobbing above water until school started. Enrolling in summer classes had been a terrible mistake. I had so much homework that I could hardly keep my head above water.

There I go with the water metaphors again. I must be thirsty. The only thing in the refrigerator is day-old milk—that I promptly dumped down the sink—and an assortment of half-empty salad dressings. Plain tap water it is. What's the point of Aunt Rhoda staying with me if she can't even pitch in for groceries once in a while?

My Women in Literature homework wasn't inspiring me, but I knew that if I threw in the towel and tried to go to sleep I'd regret it. There's a full moon tonight and I wonder if its pull on the tides is what has me feeling restless right down to my bones.

The Thornton's fridge is always stocked with every kind of soda and juice imaginable. I don't know who drinks all of it, but it's always fresh and never beyond the expiration date printed on the can or bottle. I suppose if I had a staff of housekeepers, my fridge would be perpetually stocked, too. I can't imagine ever being wealthy enough to where I didn't have to go grocery shopping for myself or make my own bed...

"Come on in, Car! The water's warm!"

Josh's voice called out to me and I let the wonderful sound of it wrap around me like a warm, fuzzy blanket in winter.

He was already neck-deep in the lake and I was standing on the shore, my toes not quite touching the water. Even though I was wearing a bathing suit I still had my shoes on. When I looked closer, I saw that they weren't my usual flip-flops or Converse, they were Josh's shoes—the expensive athletic sneakers his mom had given him for Christmas last year.

"C'mon, Car!" Josh urged from his spot in the lake. His head bobbed up and down as he pushed out into deeper water.

My feet stubbornly remained on the shore, frozen in place, immovable in Josh's neon green shoes.

The next time I looked up at him, he was even further from the shore, his chin and lips submerged in the water now.

"Josh?"

When he tried to answer me, water filled his mouth and he sank deeper until all I could see was his forehead and the top of his head.

I wanted to dive in after him, I really did. But my feet wouldn't move, no matter how hard I tried to lift them.

Besides, I was too tired to chase him any longer and it was so warm and cozy here.

By the time I lifted my dreary eyes to the water again, Josh had gone all the way under. He hadn't fought it. Hadn't caused the water to ripple or churn. He'd simply let himself sink down, down, down…

I woke up gasping for air, a thin sheen of sweat covering my body.

"Josh," I panted, his name still fresh on my lips from the dream.

But he wasn't here. He wasn't drowning in August Lake either. And I wasn't wearing his shoes.

I looked down at my bare feet and shook off the remnants of the dream. As I untangled the sheet from around my legs I tried to think of something else, hoping that the dream would fade into the background in my mind. If you distracted yourself enough and didn't replay them over and over, dreams usually disappeared from your memory as if they'd never happened.

An hour later, when I got to Josh's, I thought I saw a head bobbing in the water beyond the dock. Knowing it was a mirage, I squeezed my eyes shut, counted to ten, and then slowly opened them again. The only thing on the lake was a pair of mallards dabbling along the surface of the water for food.

The memory of the dream might have started to fade away, but the sound of Josh's voice rang in my ears for the rest of the day.

Day 53

Josh. There are a few things I think you should know. One of them is that no matter what happens, I will wait for you. However long it takes for you to do whatever you have to do, I will be here for you. I just hope you figure it out soon because I really want to go to college. And I don't think I could concentrate on my schoolwork with you still here. Or there. Or wherever it is you are inside your brain.

Another thing I think you should know is that I love you, Josh. I've loved you since the very first time we met in fifth grade when you picked me for dodgeball when no one else would.

And the next day we played Amoeba Tag and had to hold hands with a partner.

I'd never held hands with a boy before that day—and suddenly our teacher was requiring it in the name of education. After that day, I didn't want to hold hands with anyone but Josh.

I can remember it so clearly. Josh had laced his fingers through mine like a boyfriend would. Then he gave my hand a firm squeeze. Surprised, I looked over at him, not sure what expression I'd find on his face. He was grinning, my favorite crooked smile, his eyes all aglow, anticipating the competition of the game. I smiled back and never looked at another boy the same way since.

I know the way we met is not the most romantic story, but it means something to me. Ever since that day-even though your dodgeball team lost-we've been the best of friends. We made so many memories together. And I've cherished every single one of them.

It feels like we've lived a lifetime together, but believe me, Josh, there is so much more life to live. So much left to experience. So many more memories to make. I don't want you to miss out on a single second of it. You've missed out on a lot this summer, but I can't wait to make up for lost time with you.

We're going to have a wonderful future. And even when the bad junk messes stuff up, we'll get through it together the same way we got through this little rough patch. It won't be easy, but it'll be a little bit more bearable with you by my side.

I don't want you to miss out anymore. I want to tell you to take whatever time you need, but I'm also selfish and want to shake you until you wake up because I miss you so much.

I miss you, Josh.

I feel like I've grown so much this summer. I've done things I never would have done-thanks to you-and I'd do anything to get you to come back to us. Come back to me, Josh.

Come back.

I miss your laugh and your silly jokes and the way you know just how to cheer me up when I need it. I need you here to cheer me up, Josh.

Nothing is the same without you—not that I ever thought it would be.

Come back, Josh. I'm here waiting for you.

Always and forever.

Chapter Five

Day 56

Holy cow, Josh! You're not going to believe this!
I won you a hat!

Yep, you read that right. Several weeks ago, when
Midway Market had a drawing for a Razors hat, I
entered both of our names. To my surprise, your name
was drawn and you are now the proud owner of a
special, limited edition Razors hat.

Truthfully, I'd forgotten all about the drawing. I had
entered so long ago that I figured someone else had won or
they'd scrapped the giveaway altogether. But when I was in the
store this morning buying cereal, Abram, the owner, looked at
me with this big grin on his face.

"Carli, we'd like to present you with the prize hat on
Josh's behalf," he said happily.

I couldn't believe it. We'd won! Josh would be ecstatic to
add another hat to his collection.

I ran the pads of my fingers over the red hat's bill and
smiled. I hoped the universe was doing some foreshadowing of
its own.

I wouldn't have done half the things I did that summer if it
wasn't for Josh. When there a meteor shower in June, I
went down to the shore with Gordie and lay on my back and
watched the sky. I probably would have just watched from the
window in Josh's room, but I knew that had he been awake, he

would have gone outside and done the same thing. He didn't live his life by looking through a window. He went out and did things and cherished every minute of it.

So, with that in mind, I set out on another adventure with me, myself and I.

CoLa—that's what everyone who followed Razors hockey called team captain Cody Lambert—was signing autographs in Red Valley. CoLa didn't make a lot of appearances, so who knew when the next opportunity would be to see him. How awful would Josh feel if he woke up and found out he'd missed out on seeing his idol in person?

I had to lie to Aunt Rhoda and tell her I was going to the library to study for a test, but it was well worth that little niggling guilt I felt in my stomach.

I took a bus to Red Valley and walked the rest of the way to the Razors' Merchandise Store. When I arrived, the line of people went out the door and all the way around the side of the building. I had gotten there early, but obviously not early enough. If I didn't know better, I'd think that half of the state had turned out to see CoLa.

As we inched along, everyone in line chattered about Cody and about games they had attended in the past. Josh and I had gone to quite a few Razors games together and there was nothing like watching him cheer for his favorite team. Josh took every game seriously, like the fate of the world was at stake during each one. He'd get all tense when the puck was in possession of the Razors and he wasn't satisfied until they finally scored a goal. And then the other team would turn around and score and the struggle would start all over again.

Josh really would have loved this. He would have stood in line with me, talking about Cody and the rest of the Razors to whoever would listen. Instead, I stood quietly in line by myself, trying to come up with something to say to Cody that didn't sound completely lame.

Looking around, I didn't see Mark or any of Josh's other friends. Probably because they'd ended up going to Six Flags like they'd been talking about all summer. Josh would have forgone the trip to the amusement park because he'd say he could ride a roller coaster any old time. There were only a few limited dates that Razors players made public appearances and did autograph signings. Josh had his priorities.

Slowly but surely, the line moved and everyone filed inside. Cody Lambert was seated behind a table on the far wall. He looked even taller and bigger in person than he did on TV and from up in the stands at games. He had broad shoulders and his muscular arms peeked out of his T-shirt sleeves. He was handsome and appeared to be friendly. All the things you'd expect a professional athlete to be.

He patiently took photos with fans, shook hands, and signed everything that was handed to him—everything from books to hockey sticks to action figures.

When it was finally my turn, it sunk in how wrong it felt to be there without Josh. This was *his* thing. This was something he'd talk about for weeks. And after it was all over, he'd talk about it for a few more weeks.

Cody was Josh's favorite player and I was simply the messenger. Josh had really better wake up after *this*.

It would have been easy to be intimidated by a man like Cody, but he wore an easy smile that reassured me he wouldn't bite. He looked extra handsome in his street clothes without all of his hockey gear. It's weird how a hockey legend could look so much like a regular person. If you saw him on the street and didn't know who he was you'd think he was just a normal guy—who went to the gym *a lot*.

Stepping up to the table he was seated behind, I cleared my throat. It was now or never. "Hi," I said, croaked really.

Cody didn't seem to mind the one-word greeting. He said hi back and smiled. As he reached for the hat, I was blinded by the fancy Cartier watch on his wrist and his platinum wedding band. His accessories probably cost more than my house.

His pen scribbled out his signature and I was momentarily mesmerized by the muscles in his arms. In a moment of bravery, I asked him to take a photo with me and the hat. I was shaking I was so nervous. But when you were doing something for someone else's benefit, I had discovered you could do just about anything.

"It's for my friend Josh," I explained about the hat. I gave CoLa Josh's hockey card of him to sign, too. "He's in a coma. You're his favorite player and I know he'd be here to meet you if he could."

Even though the words all rushed together, Cody seemed to understand me well enough. His brows drew together and he got a concerned look on his face. He was probably thinking how he hoped to God nothing tragic like that ever happened to one of his own kids. I knew Cody had a few of his own because Josh was always telling me what a good dad he must be.

"He travels a lot, though," I had pointed out to Josh. "He's probably barely ever home during the season."

"Yeah," Josh had said, sounding disappointed. "I guess so."

I think Josh merely liked the idea of having a dad who was around to spend time with him.

Cody took a promotional card from the stack on the table, signed it as well, and handed it to me along with the hat. "Sorry to hear about your friend. Call me when he wakes up and I'll drop by for a visit."

I knew the Razors visited the children's hospital occasionally and I hoped Josh's idol would stay true to his word.

"Thanks," I murmured, a little shocked and a lot star-struck.

Cody proceeded to write his phone number in my notebook. It was a manly scrawl, but the numbers were legible.

All this time I knew the journal would come in handy one day. I liked to keep all my hockey players' phone numbers together in a safe place.

With the hat clutched close to my body, I walked out into the summer sun missing Josh more than ever.

Day 60

As I wrote the number in the journal, I couldn't believe Josh had been in a coma for two full months. Not only did it sound like forever, but it *felt* like forever, too.

Determined not to dwell on the negative, I told Josh the exciting news...

Cody Lambert was at the Razors store signing autographs today. I know he's your favorite hockey player of all time and you'd kick yourself if you missed it, so I went down and got his autograph for you. You're welcome.

There were so many people lined up to see him you'd think he was Elvis or something. I told him the autograph was for you and that you were in a coma. He said he hoped you were better soon. (Exact words). He was really nice and not scary to meet in person at all.

I even had him take a selfie with me. I figured you'd want proof so you wouldn't think I chickened out and took a Magic Marker to your hat and signed his name.

Cody also said he'd visit you when you woke up. (Yeah, we're on a first name basis now.)

If that wasn't incentive enough to wake Josh up, then I didn't know what was.

Chapter Six

Throughout the past few weeks, Aunt Rhoda had come and gone as she pleased. For someone who didn't stick around for more than a couple days, she sure took it upon herself to butt into every aspect of my life. She was currently draped across my couch, eating the last of the chips and salsa I had bought for my dad. All that criticizing must work up an appetite. Luckily, Dad had called me last night to tell me he was coming home the day after tomorrow.

Aunt Rhoda didn't do much besides watch TV, so when she made a phone call that night, I knew I was in for a rare treat. What rubbed me the wrong way was the fact that she was using our landline. Probably racking up long-distance charges for my dad to pay.

I didn't hear the first part of her conversation because she had the program she was watching turned up to eardrum-bursting decibels. When she finally turned the volume down and I edged out of my room far enough to where she couldn't see me, I could hear her clearly.

And then immediately wished I couldn't.

"I heard the Thornton's are going to finally pull the plug." Her pretentious tone suggested she was an authority on the subject and that couldn't be further from the truth.

She nodded, like the person on the other end could see her. "Uh-huh. I heard he's sucking them dry financially and they can't afford to keep him alive."

Anger blasted through me and my hands started to shake. Followed by my knees.

My first instinct was to storm into the living room, rip the phone from Rhoda's ear and give her a carefully worded piece of my mind.

Fear won out and I slipped back into my room on wobbly legs. Something about Rhoda's ignorant words struck a chord of terror deep inside my gut. The what-ifs fired up in my brain again and I realized that my worst fear had a possibility of actually happening.

And I hated Aunt Rhoda for reminding me of that disturbing fact.

I had to see Catherine in person. She'd tell me the words I needed to hear. Gossip might be petty and trivial, stupid and pointless, but sometimes there was an amount of truth to it. And the truth was what I was running after tonight.

I shoved my feet into my shoes and went out the back door as quietly as I could. The sun had already disappeared behind the mountains and it was getting dark. Riding my bike on the street at night probably wasn't the smartest thing to do, but my safety was the last thing on my mind. All I could think about was seeing Josh and making sure he was still alive.

Pulling the plug.

I pedaled until my legs burned.

There was no telling what Vulture Face would do if she found out I was AWOL. But that was a risk I was willing to take.

Pulling the plug.

It wasn't like there was an actual plug to pull—Josh didn't need a ventilator to breathe anymore—but there *were* feeding tubes.

Pulling the plug.

What a horrible image. Josh wasn't some machine hooked up to a battery. He wasn't an artificial lifeform plugged in to the mainframe computer. He was Josh Thornton, a human being. A human freaking being. The only thing "plugged" into him was an IV of fluids. The IV was his nutrition. His lifeline in a bag.

And Catherine had the power to have it taken away from him.

Josh would tell me I was being crazy.

"They aren't going to pull the plug on me, Car," he'd say. *"They know I'm still in here."*

The whole ride there, I kept in the shadows, which wasn't difficult to do at that hour in the evening. I wasn't even pedaling that hard anymore, but Aunt Rhoda's conversation had my heart beating extra fast and my breath huffing out. Anger and fear swirled inside me.

Helplessness overwhelmed me. And I swiftly tamped it down and focused on thinking only positive thoughts. Lately, the positives were few and far between. Fortunately, I was too stubborn to let the negatives plunge me into the swirling darkness.

When I reached the Thornton's, I dumped my bike on the walkway and barged into the house through the front door. I found Mrs. T in the living room, flipping through a magazine.

"Are you planning on pulling the plug on Josh?" I was out of breath, but I pushed the words out of my mouth, afraid that if I didn't act quickly, she'd pull the plug right out from under me.

Catherine looked at me like an extra head had sprouted out of my neck. "I will do no such thing!"

"What about *Mr*. T?" Josh's mom wasn't the only variable here.

"Over my dead body," she said vehemently.

"I'm sorry. It's just that I heard someone talking—"

"Carli, what an awful thing to ask me." She stood up from the sofa, wobbled a bit, and then sat back down again. "It's none of anyone's *damn* business what goes on with my son."

"I'm sorry," I repeated. Time was of the essence and there was no delicate way to broach the subject. "If you ever decided to, would you tell me first?"

She shook her head. "It's not ever going to happen."

"Do you promise?" I needed something more than her word. I needed it in writing, etched in stone and displayed behind glass.

"*Carli.*"

"What about financially?" I didn't care what lines I was crossing. I had to know.

"Frankly, Carli, my family's finances are none of your business. Even if we were bankrupt, which I assure you we are *not*, we'd still care for Josh."

My shoulders slumped from exhaustion. "Okay."

I let out the breath I'd been holding and swiped my hand over my face. My cheeks were wet, but I didn't remember commanding any tears to fall. I blinked up at the ceiling in an attempt to keep them at bay.

Catherine had fought to have Josh brought home when the doctors advised against it, I reminded myself. She'd hired her own doctor and had Josh brought home. She wouldn't give up on him so easily. If it weren't for Rhoda I never would have assumed Catherine might.

"Okay," I said again, more to calm myself down than to reassure Catherine that everything was indeed all right. "I need to see Josh."

Catherine nodded and reached for the wine glass on the coffee table in front of her.

I jogged up the stairs and into Josh's room. Agatha looked up from the book she was reading. Every day she greeted me with a smile, but tonight she frowned. "What's wrong, child?"

I was out of breath from the stairs and the fear. She got up and ushered me to the window seat, but I refused to sit down. "I need to see Josh."

"He's right here, honey," she assured me. "He hasn't gone anywhere since you left this afternoon."

I rushed to his bedside and took his hand in mine, not caring for once if we had onlookers. Agatha discreetly left the room.

Wake up, dammitt! I screamed inside my head. I didn't say the words out loud. Josh had heard me say them enough times by now.

Tears burned my eyes and I let them fall down my face and drip from my cheeks.

"Open your eyes and look at me," I whispered brokenly. "*Please.*"

A tear landed on the white sheet, turning it gray. It wasn't the first tear I had cried for Josh. And for myself. They came when I least expected them to and seemed like a nuisance more than anything.

Why did humans cry anyway? Was it to let everyone around them know they were sad? Whatever the reason, it seemed pointless. Especially shedding them for someone who couldn't even see them.

I suppose not all tears are sad tears. Some people cried when they were really happy.

Tonight, my tears were definitely of the sad variety.

Gordie thought I was being crazy. He whined at me and pawed at my leg. With my free hand, I hugged the frightened dog close to me.

Josh remained motionless. If he was going to wake up, this would be the ideal time. I needed him more than ever and I didn't want to face everything alone anymore.

Minutes passed and Josh still didn't wake up. I began to severely doubt his dedication to our friendship.

Since I was at the Thornton's for the nurse's shift change, Agatha offered me a ride home. I was rarely still at Josh's this late and I had a feeling Aunt Rhoda would find out about me sneaking out and make my life even more miserable than it already was. If that was even possible. I silently dared her to try.

I accepted Agatha's offer and put my bike in the back of her pickup truck. Agatha drove me to my house in silence. Most likely, she'd heard my conversation with Catherine and didn't want to say anything. Or she simply didn't know what to say.

I spent most of the ride home imagining what kind of punishment a woman like Aunt Rhoda could dream up for me.

"Something have you upset?" Agatha's voice rescued me from an imagined fate that involved dungeons and dank prisons.

"Huh? Oh. Yeah, I guess." I fiddled with the seatbelt for a few seconds before sucking in a deep breath and finally telling her the truth. "My aunt is staying at my house and she's being a royal pain. She said...she said some stuff about Josh tonight and I couldn't sleep without saying goodnight to him."

Agatha nodded, keeping her eyes on the road. "He's real lucky to have a friend like you."

Although I smiled at the compliment, my heart hurt a little. "Everyone thinks I'm crazy."

"Love is a crazy thing, honey."

I didn't even have to tell her exactly what I was talking about. She just knew. She knew I loved Josh with all of my heart and all of my soul and he didn't even know it.

"Don't forget to take some time for yourself once in a while," she advised.

"I will," I said automatically. Time with Josh *was* time for myself.

When Agatha parked in front of my house, I lingered in the truck, reluctant to face my aunt's vicious wrath. Reluctant to face reality, too. And my own loneliness.

Agatha reached over and squeezed my knee. "It's going to be okay, sweetie. One way or another, everything is going to work out for the best."

Right then I came to a realization. Women like Agatha were the kind of adults I should be hanging out with. Not people who were in a big hurry to pull the plug on any sign of life—and humanity. Not people like Kendall and Sierra who thought that illness was creepy.

Fortunately, not everyone was like Rhoda and Kendall and Sierra. Some people were kind and caring and sympathetic. Like Agatha. Too bad that kind of person wasn't waiting for me on the porch with folded arms and a scowling frown.

I thanked Agatha for the ride, told her I'd see her tomorrow, and got my bike out of the back. The pickup zoomed away, leaving me to face the dragon.

"Where did you go?" Aunt Rhoda demanded. Her foot tapped impatiently on the ground.

If I thought her face was pointy before, I'd never seen it when she was angry.

"I was just putting my bike away for the night." I really needed to work on my lying. The excuse sounded so flimsy and weak that I feared she could see right through me. But until she had shown up, I hadn't had much need for telling lies.

"You are not to leave this house without getting permission from me first."

I lifted my shoulders in a shrug.

"You are to answer me when I speak to you," she snapped.

"Yes ma'am," I drawled.

I marched up the steps and swerved around her on the porch.

"Oh and by the way," I said over my shoulder. "Mr. and Mrs. Thornton have no intention of pulling the plug on their son. I thought you'd want to know so you can tell the whole town."

I stomped inside, wondering how my mom's Sicilian temper hadn't gotten me into more trouble before now.

Chapter Seven

In the morning when I was waiting for my Pop-Tarts to pop out of the toaster, I thought I heard a noise outside. I was halfway through my frosted strawberry when I heard it again. Something was scratching at the back door.

Then I heard barking.

"Gordie?"

When I opened the door and saw Gordie standing there looking anxious, practically dancing on his four hairy legs, I had to swallow my breakfast back down. He must have gotten out through the doggie door in Josh's mudroom.

Gordie barked again.

Something was wrong with Josh. I could feel it in my bones. Why else would Gordie leave his post? He knew it was his job to guard Josh. Wasn't there a cat who could tell when a person had cancer? Maybe Gordie knew something we didn't. Maybe he knew that I was the best person to alert if something went wrong. Because I was the one person who was prepared to fight for Josh, tooth and nail, if anything were to happen.

I grabbed my backpack off the kitchen chair and rushed outside. Gordie took off in a sprint in the direction of Josh's house.

Every once in a while I wished I had a driver's license and a car. This was one of those times. Although, I probably wouldn't have been any more stable driving a car right now as opposed to riding my bike. Texting was impossible to do through the handlebars, so I just kept pedaling as fast as humanly possible and hoped for the best. Anyway, it was better I found out what was going on after I was on flat ground again and not wobbling on two wheels.

Not only was Mamie surprised to see me so early in the morning, but the way I burst into the room as if hellhounds were chasing me obviously startled the nightshift nurse.

Dropping my backpack on the floor, I made a beeline for Josh. Normally, his cheeks were pale, but today his skin was flushed and red splotches covered his skin. "What happened?"

"He has a fever. I already called Dr. Patel. He's on his way."

I took Josh's hand in mine and his skin was clammy. I kissed his wrist, his knuckles, his fingertips. If I was violating him, I didn't care. This might be my last chance—

No! I wouldn't think like that. I *couldn't* think like that. It was just a fever. He'd had one before, when he'd been in Intensive Care. He had pulled through it then and there was no doubt in my mind that he'd do it again now.

"Why didn't you call me?" I asked frantically.

"Because it's low-grade."

"What does that mean?" Why didn't I know about this stuff already? I'd need to beef up my medical studies.

"It's above normal, but not higher than 100.4 F," Mamie explained. "As long as it's below 104 there's nothing to worry about."

Easy for her to say. Worry had become my new best friend this summer.

I leaned down and whispered in his ear. "You can fight this, Josh. *Fight through it*. I'm here with you, fighting by your side every step of the way."

This couldn't be how it ended. What about his hopes and dreams? What about his dream to play for the Razors one day? Or his plans to travel around the world and visit every hockey arena in the UNHL? There was so much he hadn't been able to do. So much he wanted to accomplish. He just needed time. He needed a second chance.

He just needed to wake up.

I looked around and was surprised to find that Mamie and I were the only ones in the room. "Where's Mrs. T?" I asked her.

A look of unease flashed in her eyes. "She went downstairs to call Mr. T."

A few long minutes later, when Mrs. T still didn't return, I tore myself away from Josh and went downstairs to find Catherine and find out why she was avoiding her son.

I followed the trail of light coming from the kitchen. Josh's mom was leaning against the sink, a glass in her hand. An empty bottle of pomegranate-flavored vodka sat on the counter next to her.

She glanced up and saw me standing in the doorway. Her eyes looked right through me like I wasn't even there. She couldn't see me there in front of her. All she could see was her own grief, muddled by her debilitating addiction.

I didn't know what to say. Josh was upstairs fighting for his life and his mom was finishing off a bottle of vodka like her life depended on it.

She looked at me with red, puffy eyes and fat tears streaked down her face, causing her mascara to run. "We're losing him, Carli. He's dying."

"No, we're not," I argued. "He just has a low-grade fever."

As long as it's below 104 there's nothing to worry about.

Catherine shook her head and staggered. She held onto the counter to keep from swaying.

I went to her. I knew we were feeling some of the same emotions, but I wouldn't give in so easily. I couldn't fully understand what it must be like to be a mother and see your son injured, but I knew what it was like to see my best friend struggling.

We couldn't afford to show weakness. We couldn't give up on him.

"Let's go sit with him," I told her gently. "He *needs* us."

She reeked of liquor, like her skin couldn't contain it all and it was seeping through her pores.

"No! I can't see him like this anymore." She gulped down the rest of her vodka. She turned to set the empty glass on the counter, but her shaky hand missed and it hit the marble floor and shattered.

We both looked at the broken glass scattered on the stone floor.

"I'm so tired, Carli." Catherine looked at me with heartbreakingly hollow eyes before covering her face with her hands. Sobs shook her small frame.

Oh no. I wasn't prepared to deal with her crying. I was here to help her fight for her son.

Hesitating, I put my hand on her shoulder to comfort her and was surprised by how bony she felt through the thin satin robe she was wearing. She'd been practically wasting away these past few months, replacing nutrition with alcohol. Who had been watching over her while I had been watching over Josh?

No one.

She sobbed some more and I grabbed a paper towel for her to wipe her face with. Instead of dabbing it beneath her eyes, she balled it into her fist and cried some more. Sobs wracked her body.

"Here, let me help you up to bed."

It wasn't like she was my mom or I had any obligation to her, but it was something Josh would have done. He would have made a joke about it and helped her upstairs because that's the kind of person he was. *Is*.

Mumbling incoherently, Catherine leaned on me and we hobbled up the stairs together. The going was slow, but I finally maneuvered her into the master bedroom. In the dark, the light switch was difficult to locate. After what seemed like an awkwardly long time, I finally found it and switched it on. Suddenly the room was bathed in soft yellow light.

Mr. and Mrs. T's bedroom was full of rustic yet chic hickory furniture. They had really taken the lodge décor idea and ran with it. A massive stone fireplace stood guard in the corner. Opposite the fireplace was a giant four post bed. Oversized furniture filled the room and seemed to swallow up the space. Instead of warm and cozy, it all looked rather intimidating to me.

On the far side of the room, the wall of windows that looked out over the lake was covered by heavy drapes. When open, the view mirrored the one in Josh's room. Apparently Catherine wasn't fond of letting sunlight into her room either.

"You should be at home taking care of your own mother," Catherine slurred.

Apparently in her inebriated state, she had forgotten that my mother had died. I didn't appreciate the harsh reminder.

"Where is your husband, Catherine? Where's Warren?" How could the loss of one person tear an entire family apart so brutally?

"Denver...er Chicago...don't remember which." She shook her head, her whole body flopping against mine. "Don't need him."

"Yes, but Josh does."

"Am glad you're Josh's girlfriend," she murmured, ignoring me.

Her words made me freeze. And then I shook off the shock and kept moving. A bottle of vodka did wonders for the human mind.

"Sometimes I wish it was you instead of my Josh."

Her words should have been like a slap to the face, but I found myself agreeing with her.

Me, too, I solemnly thought to myself. Me, too.

After pulling the bedspread and sheet aside, I sat her down on the bed and removed her slippers. Her polished pedicure was a stark contrast to the troubled woman beneath. On the outside, she appeared to have it all. A new car, designer clothes, a home most people only dreamed of…

But wealth wasn't everything. Her youngest son's life was slowly being sucked away from him and no amount of money or Prada handbags could change that.

For the first time in my life, I felt sorry for Catherine Thornton. Despite her country club membership, her fabulous wardrobe and her wealthy husband, she was completely alone. She didn't have any friends or loved ones helping her through this ordeal. She'd navigated her way this far with the help of her 100 proof companions.

"Do you think I'mma bad muther?" She swung her legs up onto the bed, nearly smacking me in the face. I ducked just in time.

"Huh, Car*lin*a?" She enunciated the syllables in my name like it was her new favorite game.

So, suddenly she'd decided it was a good time to become talkative, huh? The last thing I wanted to do was have a conversation with someone who probably wouldn't remember it when she woke up.

"No," I answered through clenched teeth. "I think you need to get some sleep."

"Yer a nice girl, Cuhreeleena."

Had Josh put his mother to bed like this in the past? He'd never mentioned anything about her drinking, but I could see now why he wouldn't have. As close as we were, he wouldn't want anyone knowing about her shameful secret.

When Catherine was situated in bed, I pulled the covers up to her chin.

She looked at me, her glassy eyes blinking heavily. "Don't tell Josh 'bout this."

"I won't," I answered.

Then I turned off the light and pulled the door closed behind me.

Back downstairs, I found a broom and dustpan and swept up the broken glass in the kitchen.

The tiny shards of glass were a metaphor for so many things. The past…memories, Josh and I growing up together… The future…any hope Josh had of playing hockey again, graduation, Senior Prom, college—all the things we probably wouldn't get to experience together.

Upstairs, Agatha had taken Mamie's place and my favorite RN reassured me that Josh's fever was indeed low-grade and that worrying was unnecessary.

A short time later, when Dr. Patel arrived, his calm presence soothed both Agatha and me. These were bewildering times for us and we needed someone with compassion—as well as an office full of degrees and awards—on our side.

Dr. Patel's credentials were a mile long and he was the smartest man I'd ever met. I looked up to a man like him. Someone who had a gentle bedside manner, was kind, and took the time to explain the complicated, often confusing world of medicine to a naïve teenager like me. He didn't have to explain things in layman's terms until I understood them. But he did. He *cared*. And for that I didn't know how to repay him.

"Where is Catherine?" Dr. Patel asked me when he finished examining Josh.

"She's…indisposed. And Mr. Thornton is out of town on business." Agatha had informed me that Warren was in Chicago for business and wouldn't be back until tomorrow. With Josh's family otherwise occupied, it was up to me to supervise his care.

"Is Josh going to be all right?" I asked Dr. Patel.

Dr. Patel gave me a warm smile that was meant to calm my nerves. "The fever hasn't spiked and that's an encouraging sign."

I nodded, knowing there wasn't much more he could tell me. It must be frustrating to have all those degrees and still not be able to know what was going on inside a coma patient's mind.

Dr. Patel started to walk away and then turned back to me. "You are incredibly astute, Carli. Josh is fortunate to have you looking out for him."

I managed a weak smile in return. "Thank you."

I watched him walk away and thanked my lucky stars that Josh had a doctor as intelligent and kind as Dr. Patel.

The fever clung to Josh all through the night. I stayed by his side and let the nurses do their thing. First Agatha and then Mamie after the shift change. Not once did I stop whispering words of encouragement into his ear.

Hours later, as I drifted off to sleep in the chair beside Josh's bed, I thought about Catherine and how Warren was in Chicago and how my dad was on a freeway somewhere. The men in our life weren't where they were supposed to be. And the women were barely holding on.

"Carli?" A distorted voice penetrated the heavy haze of my sleep. Without opening my eyes, I tried to place who it belonged to.

"Carli?"

There it was again. The voice was familiar and…

It was Josh! He'd woken up!

Shoving myself awake, I blinked and looked up. A face hovered over me, blurry and unrecognizable. I blinked again. No, it wasn't Josh. The voice belonged to Agatha. Agatha was with me and Josh was still asleep.

"Your dad's downstairs," she was telling me.

"My *dad's* here?"

"Yes, honey. Your dad's here."

I sat up and rubbed the sleep from my eyes. Something warm was covering me and I realized Mamie had put a throw blanket over me sometime during the night.

"How's Josh?" I asked, tossing the blanket aside.

Agatha smiled and it was a welcome sight compared to the hard edge of concern her face had worn earlier. "The fever is gone."

"Oh, good! I thought—" I choked on the rest of the words, too afraid to finish the sentence.

I leaned over the bed and put my palm over Josh's hand. It wasn't clammy anymore. His skin was back to its normal paleness. No more red splotches. No more fever.

The weight was lifted from my shoulders and I could breathe easily again.

His vitals are good.

Before heading downstairs, I used the bathroom and splashed some cold water on my face. There was a kink in my neck and my back was sore from falling asleep in the chair. I ran a brush through my hair and dug the rest of the crusties out of my eyes.

What was my dad doing here? The question swirled around inside my head as I gathered up my backpack and said goodbye to Agatha.

As I made my way down the stairs I saw my dad standing in the foyer. He crossed his arms, uncrossed them crossed them over his chest again. He looked as out of place here as a grizzly bear at the Hilton.

My dad was a big guy. He wasn't obese or anything, although he could have been from sitting in a truck all day, but he was stout and muscular. Everyone was intimidated by him until they got to know him. And when they did, it didn't take long for them to realize he was a teddy bear on the inside.

I guess his scruffy beard made him seem unapproachable to some people. He'd let his facial hair grow after Mom died. It had tickled her when they kissed, so he'd always kept his face clean shaven.

"Dad? What are you doing here?" I asked when I reached the bottom of the stairs.

He looked over at me, his expression a mixture of embarrassment and relief.

I closed the space between us and hugged him tight, soaking up his strength and stability.

Before he could answer my question, Rita the Thornton's housekeeper, swept into the room. "Are you *sure* I can't get you a glass of tea or something? A sandwich perhaps?" she asked sweetly. Lord knows, Rita had fed me more sandwiches than I could count.

"No, but thanks." Dad cleared his throat and turned his attention back to me. "I'm just here to see if Carli would like to go have breakfast."

"I could go for some pancakes," I answered, smiling.

Dad didn't ask me why I had spent the night at Josh's house. He didn't have to grill me about it for me to know he cared. Not many fathers would let their teenage daughter spend the night at a boy's house, but, like Mr. and Mrs. T, Dad understood.

"Josh had a fever last night," I explained.

Dad frowned, deep lines appearing on his forehead. "How is he?"

His vitals are good.

"He fought through it and his temperature is back to normal now."

"Good."

When we went outside, I saw my dad's semi-truck parked in the circle drive. I wondered what Mrs. T would think of all that chrome and the American flag airbrushed on the sides. It wasn't a sight Catherine would want the neighbors to see. What would the Joneses think? Luckily the Thornton house sat back a ways from the road and the thick trees made it nearly impossible to see in.

Without thinking twice about it, I grabbed onto the handhold, stepped onto the foothold, and hauled myself up into the cab. I'd been climbing into one type of semi-truck or another since I could walk. The air suspension seat squeaked and joggled when I sat down. With my dad in the driver's seat, the truck rattled to life and lurched onto the main road.

In the middle of downtown, the Lion's Den Diner sat off the main road, beckoning tourists and locals alike to try their "wicked" good food. The Lion's Den was decorated in a *The Wizard of Oz* theme and we were seated in a booth beneath a giant poster of Dorothy and the Cowardly Lion.

I ordered pancakes and my dad ordered the biggest thing on the menu—the Tin Man Hearty Breakfast.

My orange juice came with a straw and I played with the paper wrapper, folding it into a mini accordion, while I waited for Dad to speak.

He scratched at his beard, looking like he wanted to crawl out of his own skin. From experience, I knew this was his signal for "I've got something to say that you're not gonna like too much."

Even though he hadn't mentioned anything yet, I was prepared to tell him that I didn't want Aunt Rhoda staying with us—*me*—anymore. My dad might have been intimidating to others, but I had no qualms about going toe to toe with him. I was smart enough to pick my battles with him and this was one I'd fight for. I would stand my ground. But first I wanted to see what he had to say. He didn't just show up at the T's to *not* tell me something.

Finally, he spoke. "I thought this would be a good place for us to talk."

"Why? So I can't cause a scene?"

He looked away and bit the inside of his cheek.

"Okay," I said calmly. "Say your piece."

He cleared his throat and looked at me again. "I want you to think about moving in with your Aunt Rhoda for a while."

My mouth hung open. I couldn't be twenty miles from Josh with no car, no driver's license. I just couldn't. The thought of not getting to see Josh every day made me—

No. I refused to entertain such an absurd idea. Even for a second. It wasn't going to happen.

Plus, Aunt Rhoda was a horrible person. Living with her 24/7 sounded a lot like purgatory.

"You need someone to look after you," Dad muttered.

I laughed, but it sounded hollow in my own ears. "I look after myself just fine."

His eyes went from looking stern to gentle. "I know, darlin', but you're alone too damn much. Kids are supposed to have *guidance.*"

"I'm not a kid, Dad," I argued. "I'm sixtee—" I stopped myself, suddenly remembering that my birthday was only two weeks away. "I'm almost seventeen years old."

"I know, baby." He murmured something under his breath about me being more of an adult than he was. "Just think about it, okay?"

I didn't need to think about my dad's suggestion to know that I one-hundred-percent didn't want to move in with Rhoda, the Queen of Darkness. I'd have to switch schools and that was out of the question. Unfortunately, I couldn't plead "But all my friends are here" because I only had one. But all my teachers were in August Lake. They provided all the guidance and friendship I needed. This was my home and I had no intention of leaving it until I went away to college.

"And you're probably spending too much time at the Thornton's," he said as an afterthought.

The way Dad worded his statement made it sound like he wasn't one-hundred percent convinced of what he was saying. Like someone else—*Rhoda*—had put the idea into his head.

"You need to get out and do something else once in a while," he added.

"What else?" I asked, practically shrieking. "I'd just be reading a book at home. What's the difference where I am? Josh and I hang out every summer. It's what we've done ever since we were little."

"Yes, but he wasn't…*asleep* then."

"Why are you—" *Rhoda* "—having such a problem with this *now*?"

"Because I'm on the road now more than ever. Will you at least *think* about staying with Rhoda?"

No. There was nothing to think about.

I stared at him, wondering how I'd gotten into this mess in the first place.

Dad continued to push. "Rhoda has a life of her own in Red Valley and I can't expect her to give everything up and stay here all the time."

"Oh, what, her houseplants are too precious to abandon?" The bitterness of my words tasted gross in my mouth, but I wasn't about to back down.

From a young age, my father had taught me to pick my battles and this was one I had no intention of giving up on. I'd get emancipated if I had to. I'd buy a car and live in it on Josh's driveway. I'd do whatever it took.

"I can see you've dug your heels in on this," Dad observed with a sigh.

It was difficult to be mad at him; he knew me so well.

"Can you blame me?" I asked. No bitterness, just complete, raw honesty.

He looked at me and tilted his head to the side, much like Josh used to do whenever I said something profound. "No, I guess not."

It sounded like the words had cost him some to say, but I was glad he was man enough to admit them to me.

And here I had a speech outlining the pros and cons (mostly cons) ready to go and everything.

Then Dad's shoulders sagged a little (which was a difficult thing to see of a man his size) and he asked, "What am I supposed to do, Lina?"

"Nothing," I answered quickly. "Can't we just keep going on like we've been doing?"

"I suppose it ain't hurtin' anybody. As long as you're okay with being alone so much."

When I opened my mouth to argue, he waved his hand in front of my face. "I know, I know, you're not alone when you're at the Thornton kid's."

It made me want to smirk every time he called Josh a kid because Josh was older than me by a few months and I felt like anything but a kid.

After we finished our breakfast and Dad paid the bill, we went outside so he could have a smoke. Every so often I'd beg him to quit and he'd try—he really did—but it didn't last for long.

"How is he doin' anyway? I mean, besides the fever yesterday. Any change?"

"His vitals are good." The canned answer felt disingenuous. Especially when I gave it to someone I loved. My dad deserved better.

"He's the same," I said, my shoulders slouching. "He did blink the other day, but the doctor said it was probably just a reflex and not necessarily a sign of improvement."

"I'm sorry, Lina."

The kind words washed over me and I let him pull me into one of his patented bear hugs. "Me too," I told him, my voice muffled by his shoulder. "But I'm never going to give up on him. Ever."

"That's my girl. Hey," he said as he pulled away and we started for the truck. "Do you wanna go on a run with me this weekend? A short one to Reno and back?"

As much as I wanted to spend time with my dad, I just couldn't leave town—and Josh—for an entire weekend.

When I was little, I used to go on runs with my dad all the time. It was like a fun sleepover, where I got to travel to new places and we'd eat too much fast-food. Seeing the interstate from high up in a truck was a great way to travel.

"It'll do you good to get out for a little while," Dad coaxed.

Sure, it might. But what if Josh woke up while I was gone? He'd think I'd abandoned him. And I couldn't let that happen.

"Maybe some other time. Like before school starts," I suggested. "Aunt Rhoda isn't going to be mad we had breakfast without her, is she?" I asked Dad, smirking.

"Rhoda went home."

I nearly choked on my own saliva. "She did?"

He nodded. "She started nagging me about these." He flicked his cigarette onto the ground and dug his boot heel into the butt. "I've been single too long to have a woman come in and tell me how to live my life."

"Yeah," I agreed. "That's *my* job."

Day 66

You had a fever yesterday. Luckily, it didn't last for too long, but it still scared the heck out of me. Dr. Patel was really nice when he was here and he even took time out of his hectic schedule to talk to me about your condition. Your parents did a good job when they chose him to be your doctor.

I had breakfast with my dad and we cleared the air about a few things. I'll tell you more about it later. Right now I need to finish my homework and then I'm going to a movie with my dad.

That night, I took my old photo album from its place on my bookshelf and slowly flipped through the yellowing pages. There were only a few photos of my mother, and in each one she looked like a movie star with her long, black hair and smiling brown eyes. Most of the photos were of me—me by myself or me with my dad—my mother had taken those, and the few that featured my mother had been taken by my dad's steady hand.

The photo that always brought a smile to my face was the one where my mom and I were wearing sunglasses and making smoochy faces at the camera.

Carlina, age 2 was written on the back in my mom's curlicue writing.

My name was a combination of my parents' names. Carl and Angelina. They had been married for seven short years. I often wonder how different my life might be if she were still alive.

In the photos my mother looked embarrassed, like she didn't want to be the focus of attention, but I don't know why. She was so young and pretty that I smoothed my thumb over the photo and wished she was here in person. There were so many questions floating through my mind that I wanted to ask her.

What had it been like to fall in love for the first time?
How did she know my dad was the right man for her?

I took one of my favorite photos out of its plastic and brought it over to my vanity—the little table with a mirror mounted above it that my parents found at a flea market—and studied myself in the reflection. My hair was the same black as my mother's but was wavy where hers was straight. Oval face, brown eyes, delicate cheekbones. All the features that were in the photo reflected in the mirror in front of me.

Taking another glance at the photo for inspiration, I brushed my hair out and parted it down the middle the same way she had worn hers. The resemblance was uncanny.

Sitting there, on the little padded stool that my mother had picked out for me long before I had memory of it, I felt closer to her than ever before. She was there in the mirror, looking back at me with the same eyes and the same hair and the same nose. Other than the discrepancy in our ages and the wave in my hair, we could have been twins.

No wonder my dad spent so much time away.

Chapter Eight

"I never should have let you move him from the hospital," Warren snarled.

"How dare you!" Catherine screeched in return.

This wasn't the first time I'd witnessed one of Josh's parents' fights, but it sure didn't get any easier to listen to them. They were downstairs in the living room, but their enraged voices traveled up the stairs, making it seem like they were in the same room with Josh and me.

If Josh had been awake when the fight erupted, he probably would have walked out the door and gone down to the lake until the tongue-lashing subsided. But because he was confined to the bed, I stayed right where I was and weathered the storm by his side.

"The only reason you wanted him brought home was so you could drink," Mr. T accused.

"Yer a liar," Mrs. T replied, slurring each word.

I wanted to turn some music on so Josh didn't have to hear them, but curiosity won out. I sat and listened as his parents ripped each other apart with their harsh words.

"…you won't leave the house. I almost wish we'd left him in the hospital. Then, at least you'd get out of the damn house once in a while."

The Thornton's had accumulated and stowed away so much anger that they mercilessly used it against each other. The situation sucked for everyone involved, but I still couldn't understand how you could take everything out on those you supposedly loved the most. Especially when they were the only ones around. Maybe they fought with each other because there was no one else around.

"Does your *girlfriend* know about your sick son?" Catherine spat in response.

"You're drunk. You don't know what you're talking about," Warren replied.

It wasn't the first time he'd used her drinking as an excuse to change the subject.

"I know you didn't go to Chicago on *business*."

"Why don't you spend more time with your son and less time worried about what *I'm* doing?"

"The Thornley girl has been doing nothing *but* talking to him for months and it hasn't made a damn bit of difference."

"Well, it's more than I can say for *you*!"

"How *dare* you question my qualifications as a mother!"

"Go sleep it off. I'm going upstairs to see my *son*."

Footsteps stomped up the stairs. Oh no! There wasn't enough time for me to bolt before Mr. T would see me. So I did the only thing I could do. I shoved my headphones into my ears so that he wouldn't know that I'd heard the argument and tried to look naïve.

Why had Josh left me here to navigate this kind of stuff by myself? He'd abandoned me and yet he was less than two feet away.

A few seconds later, Warren came into the room and sighed heavily. "Oh, hello Carli." He actually looked surprised to see me.

I pulled the headphones from my ears and smiled. "Hi, Mr. Thornton."

Warren Thornton was a good looking man—for a dad. Josh had so many of his features that I knew I was looking at the forty-year-old version of him. His sleeves were rolled up to his elbows, his tie loosened and the top two buttons of his shirt were undone.

"May I have a minute with Josh...*alone*?"

"Sure." I jumped up and shoved my stuff into my backpack. "I was just getting ready to head to class anyway."

"Summer school?"

"Yes. I'm earning college credit."

"That's great, Carli. Good for you. Josh always balked at the idea of summer school."

I couldn't help but notice how he referred to Josh in the past tense. "Yeah, I guess he does."

"He thought it was only meant for people who were flunking out."

There he went using past tense again.

"Well..." I swung my backpack over my shoulders. "I should get going. I don't want to be late for class. Professor Dodd frowns upon tardiness." Now I was starting to ramble.

"Carli?"

I turned around on the ball of my foot. "Yes, Mr. Thornton?"

"Thanks for coming by. I never see any of Josh's other friends come around."

I smiled. "No problem."

"You're always welcome here. You know that, right?"

I nodded. "Yes. I appreciate you guys letting me come over whenever to visit Josh."

I thrived on my daily visits. If I didn't have Josh to spend time with what else would I have to do? There was only so much time you could spend studying and reading.

Satisfied, Warren nodded back.

"Bye, Josh," I called over my shoulder. "I'll see you this evening."

Mr. T looked like he didn't understand why I treated Josh like he'd actually answer me back, but I did it anyway. I wasn't about to let Warren's ignorance influence how I talked to his son.

Josh and I knew how things worked around here.

Whether his parents liked it or not, we had a connection. We did before the accident and now, after everything we'd been through, it was stronger than ever.

No one would come between us. No matter how hard they tried.

Later that night, while I was lying in bed pretending to sleep, Catherine's angry words echoed in my head. They had been directed at her husband, but they resonated with me.

"The Thornley girl has been doing nothing but *talking to him for months and it hasn't made a damn bit of difference."*

I hoped my talking to Josh *did* make a difference. What if he heard me and it kept him from getting lonely and gave him a reason to keep holding on? And if not for *his* benefit, then for mine.

Growing up as an only child, I'd never had a problem with entertaining myself. But now that Josh was incapacitated, being alone was starting to get on my nerves. I mean, he was *right there*. I could reach out and touch his skin, but he didn't look at me or talk to me.

I wished there was more I could do. Josh would never settle with sitting around and waiting for something. He'd take matters into his own hands and make things happen.

Too bad my hands were tied.

The next afternoon, I had a difficult time staying awake in Economics. It wasn't that I was particularly *tired*, but the subject matter that spewed out of Professor Dodd's mouth was of absolutely no interest to me. I wasn't interested in monopolies and supply and demand.

Then what was I interested in? I asked myself.

The next day, I asked myself the same exact question while Professor Noxon, my Women in Literature professor, droned on about how Virginia Woolf's artistic innovation was in constant dialogue with the literary traditions of her male predecessors at the turn of the last century. It wasn't Professor Noxon's fault I was bored out of my gourd. The whole point of the class was to examine how women writers in the twentieth century responded to changing cultural expectations of their roles in society. But, once again, I was reexamining my interests.

Suddenly, I realized I didn't want to learn about economics or women in literature. I wanted to learn about the human brain and why and how it could simply shut the body down and take an endless slumber while it recovered from trauma. I wanted to learn how to cure leukemia and diseases and I wanted to—

Oh. My. Gosh. All of a sudden, it hit me like a hockey stick slapping full force against a puck.

I wanted to be a doctor.

It made perfect sense. I'd always had an interest in medicine. Always been curious about my mother's terminal diagnosis. And now that Josh was a living science project, I couldn't help but want to delve into the complicated world of medicine. I could study molecular mechanisms and find answers to all the things I'd been questioning about life all summer.

I almost smacked my palm against my forehead. Why hadn't I signed up for the Introduction to Neuroscience class or Biomedical Terminology? Or even Introductory Biology? That course fulfilled the requirement of two semesters of biology needed for admission to medical school.

Stupid. Stupid.

I could harp on my erroneous decisions later. Right now I was too excited.

This was it. My destiny. I wanted to work with people who had been diagnosed with one thing or another. I wanted to have patients of my own, patients to look after and help plan their course of treatment. I wanted to be the one wearing the stethoscope, spouting knowledge about anything and everything. I wanted to be like Dr. Patel.

I had the grades and the brains and the determination. There was no reason I couldn't make it a reality.

A doctor.

Huh. More and more I liked the sound of that title.

Oh, what a day for such a revelation!

When I got home, I couldn't wait to tell my dad the news. In the past, he'd suggested I become an accountant because then at least I'd always have one client—him. But I had a sneaking suspicion that he wouldn't be disappointed in me changing future career paths.

"Dad, there's something I need to tell you. I don't want to study literature or economics. I mean, I'll finish out my summer classes, but those aren't the subjects I want to study in college." I paused for dramatic effect and then let 'er rip. "I want to go to medical school. I want to be a doctor."

He got this funny look on his face and then he blinked rapidly, his eyes looking all glassy.

"I want to learn more about the kind of cancer Mom had. And I want to understand what's happening to Josh. I think I could be really great at it."

"Oh, Lina." His voice was sort of gravelly—well, more gravelly than normal anyway—and if I didn't know better, I'd think he was going the cry.

"Are you mad?"

Even if he was, I had made up my mind. He'd warm up to my decision eventually. If he strongly objected, then I'd just have to use the powers of persuasion to convince him otherwise. I could do this. I could work hard and become a wonderful doctor.

"Oh, Lina," he said again and came toward me with open arms. "You make me so damn proud."

Carl Thornley wasn't the type of man to show emotion and I felt some of my own welling up in my throat when he wrapped me up in a giant vice-like bear hug.

Chapter Nine

The next evening when I got home from visiting Josh, Mark was sitting on my front porch. My dad had taken the run to Reno and no one was home to greet my gentleman callers.

"Carli, hi." Mark sounded surprised—or relieved—to see me and I wondered how long he'd been sitting there, waiting for me to come home.

He was dressed in the same type of clothes he always wore—a red T-shirt with the Razors logo emblazoned on the front and cargo shorts—but it looked like he had spent a little extra time taming his curly hair. I was flattered, but that didn't change the platonic way I felt about him.

"Hey." Dipping my head to hide my face, I leaned my bike against the house. My fists clenched and unclenched. I didn't want to talk to Mark. Alone. With no escape from his pleading eyes and probing questions.

Night had fallen and left everything in shadows. Luckily I had left the porch light on so I wouldn't have to find my way up the steps in the dark.

No matter how nice Mark was, I didn't want to be in the dark with him.

Sucking in a deep breath, I went over and stood beside him and leaned over the porch railing. I couldn't sit next to him and risk him grabbing for my hand or something.

"What brings you over to the east end?" I asked. Mark's family was just as wealthy as Josh's—if not more—and I thought it might help to remind him of that fact. Just in case he'd come over here to do something crazy and act on a romantic impulse.

"I was just at Josh's and thought I'd stop by and say hi."

My head whipped around to face him. "You went to see Josh?" The shock was apparent in my reaction, but I tried to act nonchalant to disguise it.

"Yeah. Nobody was there—I mean just Josh and some nurse—so I left."

"Oh."

Would it have been easier to talk to Mark with Josh in the same room? Or here on my front porch with no one around? I didn't like the sound of either scenario.

"I was hoping you'd be there," Mark said.

"I had class and then I came straight home," I explained. "Why'd you want to see me?" It would be a lot easier if he just came right out and said what he wanted. What he was here for. Why he looked at me like he wanted us to be more than friends.

He turned toward me and I reluctantly met his gaze. His rich brown eyes looked into mine and all I wanted to do was look away.

"Do you want to go out sometime? Just the two of us."

Just the two of us. The five words every girl longed to hear.

I hadn't been too keen on going out with the group without Josh, so I really didn't like the idea of going out alone with Mark. Mark didn't give me those zany butterflies that Josh did. I had tried to push my feelings for Josh aside and let the butterflies flutter for Mark, I really had. As much as I tried to convince myself, I just didn't feel those kinds of "more than friends" feelings for him. It sure would have been a lot easier to. We could be boyfriend and girlfriend and live happily ever after, but I knew deep down that we weren't meant to be together. I wasn't desperate to be with a boy just for the sake of being with someone. So I turned him down. As gently as I knew how.

"Sorry, Mark, but I don't think that's such a good idea."

He didn't fall for it.

"Come on, Carli. Go to the downtown carnival with me tonight."

I knew it was just a ploy to get me out of the house.

"I don't know," I stalled.

I supposed I should have prepared myself for life after Josh, but I sure couldn't do that when he hadn't actually gone anywhere.

"If you end up hating being around me then I'll leave you alone."

The comment was meant to make me feel at ease, but it didn't work. It made me feel like a schmuck for turning him down in the first place.

As much as I didn't want to lead Mark on, I also couldn't stand the thought of spending another evening doing Economics homework or going over to Josh's and playing double solitaire with Agatha. My brain desperately needed a break from general equilibrium theory and the sound of Josh's life support machines. Mark was opening the door for a night of reprieve.

And at the last possible second I decided to walk through it.

"Give me a few minutes, okay?" I asked him.

"Sure."

I left Mark out on the porch—rude, I know—and hurried into the bathroom and shut the door. My reflection looked as terrified as I felt. After splashing some water on my face and running a brush through my ponytail, I felt a little more human. I was not, however, primping for a date. I would humor Mark, we'd walk through the carnival, and then he'd realize that he was the third wheel in this relationship.

The downtown carnival wasn't a big production, just a few rides and games set up in the supermarket parking lot. Red Valley had a much bigger carnival in the summer, but there was no sense in driving all the way there when I didn't want to go on this pseudo date in the first place.

Since it was only a few blocks away, we decided to walk. Well, it was more like I decided to walk and took off toward town, hoping Mark would follow me.

Our hands brushed as we walked, but thankfully he didn't reach for mine and I tried to steer clear of his. I eventually shoved my hands into my back pockets for extra assurance.

When we got to the carnival, Mark insisted on buying our tickets—even when I insisted right back that I could pay for my own—and we walked through the carnival side by side, trying to think of something to say to fill the awkward silence.

He smiled. I smiled back. And then I instantly regretted it when I saw how his face lit up in return.

What if I'd never met Josh? What if I had never hit it off with him? Would Mark have swept me off my feet tonight? Or more importantly, would I let him?

I liked to think that I still wouldn't be attracted to Mark, but then again, what did my confused teenage hormones know anyway? They were secretly in love with someone who was in a persistent vegetative state.

The crowds were jam-packed where the games were set up and Mark pressed his palm to the small of my back as we weaved through the people. I could feel the heat of his hand seep through my shirt.

Why couldn't I want this? Why couldn't I let myself fall in love with him?

Because I was already in love with someone else. Because I had been in love with Josh for as long as I could remember.

It did feel nice to get out of the house for a while. To feel life bubbling around me, talking and laughing. Little kids scrambled around us, tripping over untied laces and food wrappers on the ground. Cheerful carnival music blared out of unseen speakers and colored lights covered every surface.

"Want a pretzel?" Mark asked, his voice sounding extra cheery.

I wasn't hungry, but food might provide a welcome distraction.

The parking lot sizzled beneath our feet as we walked around the attractions, nibbling on pretzels.

"So, how are your classes going?"

"Good." I chanced a peek at Mark's face and he was looking at me expectedly. I supposed it wouldn't hurt to elaborate on my answer a little bit. "I have a lot more homework than I thought I would."

"What exactly are you studying to be?"

Only Dad and I knew the answer to that question. I hadn't had the chance to tell Josh yet. And when I finally did, I preferred him to be awake for the news.

Deciding to take a chance and live a little, I answered Mark's question truthfully. "I want to be a doctor." It felt strange to tell Mark something so personal. Something I'd only figured out myself a couple days ago.

"That sounds about right," he remarked.

"What about you?" I asked, eager to steer the subject away from me. If he misinterpreted my interest, then so be it.

"After high school, I'm going to apply for the police academy. I want to be a cop."

"Wow. That's great. You'd be good at it."

"Thanks."

Our conversation died off as we walked by the noisy dart throw and basketball toss. Mark asked if I wanted to ride on the Ferris wheel, but I declined and told him I needed to get home. My Econ homework wasn't going to complete itself.

Back at my house, I made a beeline for the porch. Agreeing to spend time with Mark hadn't been the best idea I'd ever had. We didn't have anything in common besides Josh and we had nothing to talk about. Things were awkward and weird between us and going to the carnival had only made things worse.

"That was actually kind of fun, Mark. Thanks for thinking of me." The second the words left my mouth I regretted them. That had been the completely wrong thing to say.

Mark didn't seem to mind. He followed me up the steps, looking down at his feet. When his gaze lifted and met mine, I knew I had a problem on my hands.

"Look, Mark…" I let my voice trail off, hoping he'd take the hint.

"You're waiting for Josh to wake up."

His statement had more than one meaning. I was waiting for Josh—figuratively and literally. Yes, I'd been waiting for ten weeks for Josh to regain consciousness. And yes, I was *waiting* for him. Not wanting to become romantically involved with anyone besides him.

"Yes," I said, hoping he could understand.

"What if he doesn't wake up?"

"He will."

Looking doubtful, Mark nodded. "Goodnight, Carli." There was resignation in his voice. The first I'd heard all night. "I'll see you around."

"Bye." I let myself inside, closed the door and leaned against it in dramatic fashion.

Making mistakes was inevitable. All I'd done was try to live the last hour as if Josh wasn't alive and it had been a doozy of one. As long as Josh drew breath, I would remain faithful to him. From this day forward, I wouldn't waiver from that promise.

With the volume on the TV turned down low, I plopped down at the kitchen table and tackled my mountain of homework.

That night I didn't document my "date" in the journal. There was no need for Josh to read all about it when he woke up. Besides, it wouldn't be relevant to his recovery anyway.

Professor Noxon says that every experience can be turned into a learning experience. The only thing I learned from my date with Mark was that Josh was still the only one for me.

The next time I saw Mark was at the grocery store two days later. He was with Julie Chen. She was pretty and smart with long, shiny black hair and the clearest complexion of anyone at our school. Everyone else always had at least a pimple or three. Some kids had it so bad that it looked like they had smeared Ragu all over their faces. Luckily, I only had breakouts around that time of the month.

Anyway, Mark and Julie were holding hands and looking at each other with that gooey "we're so in love" sort of way. The twinge of jealousy in my stomach caught me off guard. I wasn't jealous of her because I wanted to be with Mark, I was jealous of them for being together in general. Or maybe the fact that he was conscious was what I envied. Then again, even if Josh was awake it didn't mean we would automatically be a couple either.

I waved hello, acted like I was in a hurry, paid for my Pop-Tarts and orange juice, and got out of there as quickly as my bargain-bin flip-flops would allow.

Chapter Ten

"All right, Josh. It's time for your sponge bath," Agatha announced.

I looked up from my journal just in time to see her remove the top part of Josh's hospital gown. I'd seen his bare chest before, last summer on the lake. His skin was pale now, almost translucent to where you could see the blue veins running beneath. He was much skinnier than I'd ever seen him. He needed to wake up and eat something!

In an effort to disguise my inner turmoil, I turned my back and looked out the window. In the reflection I could make out the outlines of their bodies but nothing else. The sounds were to be expected. The splash of water as Agatha dipped the washcloth into the basin. The sound of her humming as she went about completing her task.

I'd been there in the room when Agatha had given him a sponge bath a few times before, but today I just couldn't take it. It was too much of a reminder of what freedoms Josh had lost. Privacy. Privilege. The ability to care for himself.

He was helpless, defenseless, dependent on everyone. All the things he wasn't really. While the accident hadn't taken his life, it had stripped away everything else, leaving him as a lifeless shell of who he used to be.

I had to leave. How would Josh feel knowing someone had to bathe him and cut his fingernails for him? He was practically a grown man and he couldn't even do the simplest of things.

"I'm taking Gordie for a walk," I told Agatha.

I grabbed Gordie's leash and hurried out of the room before she could say anything.

A trip to August Falls wouldn't be complete without imagining what it would feel like to be kissed by Josh. I don't know what it was about this particular place that evoked thoughts about his lips touching mine for the first time. Maybe it was how romantic this place felt, with the water plunging over the cliff, filling your ears with the deafening sound of its urgency. It could also be the ethereal feeling of the mist on your face as you glanced up at the water. Like when you're in the shower and how you can stand back from the showerhead and still feel the spray of the water.

August Falls was a place where nature made a lot of noise and a big show of being beautiful. Naturally that seemed like the perfect place to show someone how much you cared for them.

Although the trail was well-maintained, the hike down to the bottom of the falls was steep. The temperature plummeted the closer Gordie and I got to the water.

As Gordie and I passed the enormous green pool, I let myself enjoy the cool, moist temperatures in the canyon. Rays of sunlight sparkled through the Douglas fir trees and California black oak.

The path leading to the bridge over August Creek (the creek that ran from the falls to the lake) was the trail less traveled and we continued on and picked our way over the exposed tree roots snaking across the ground and around moss-covered rocks.

We walked onto the August Creek Bridge and stopped in the middle to look out over the creek. Plenty of girls had been kissed in this very same spot, but I had never been kissed at all before. The moments and firsts I planned on sharing with Josh were piling up. And, unfortunately, he wasn't getting anymore awake.

Being friends with Josh had always given me a sense of belonging that I'd never felt before. And now, being friends with Josh had isolated me from everything and everyone.

Day 75

I took Gordie to the Falls today. He's been so depressed lately that I thought it would be good for him to get out for a little while. On the way there, he kept looking back like he expected you to follow us. Even though his tongue was hanging out of his mouth, he still looked somewhat sad.

I'm not the only one who misses you, Josh.

The following day, when I pulled up to the Thornton's, I didn't recognize the white Audi Q7 in the driveway. Curiosity had me speculating as to who the luxury SUV belonged to. Who was the Thornton's mystery visitor?

Something about unexpected visitors made my insides queasy.

Inside the house, low voices came from Josh's room. Like an adolescent eavesdropper, I lingered in the mudroom, trying to identify the voices. The feminine voice belonged to Agatha—that I knew. The masculine one I couldn't quite place. It sounded so similar to Josh's that my heart flip-flopped inside my chest.

Unsure of what I'd find inside—or more accurately *who*— I rounded the corner. And saw Agatha chatting with Josh's older brother, Blake.

Blake Thornton. The prodigal son had returned home to August Lake.

I hadn't seen Blake since the early days when Josh was still in the hospital. Like a dutiful son and brother, he'd made an appearance and hung out in the waiting room of the ICU. After realizing there was nothing he could do to help his brother, Blake had gone on to continue living his life on the East Coast like nothing had happened.

And now he was standing in the middle of Josh's bedroom.

Blake wore simple khaki shorts and a white polo shirt and still managed to look like he'd walked out of a catalog for stylish men's fashion. The shirt did only an adequate job of covering his muscular arms and chest.

He was tall, handsome and obviously related to Josh. Looking at him made my heart flutter.

When I walked into the room, he looked up at me and gave me a smile that mimicked Josh's. "Carli. How are you?"

"Good. I was wondering who the SUV in the driveway belonged to."

"Yeah. I thought I'd stop by and see how things are going." Disappointment tugged on his words as he glanced over at Josh and quickly looked away again. "I'm going down to the dock for some fresh air. Wanna keep me company?"

"Okay." I didn't know if he was implying that the air in Josh's room was unbearably stuffy or that he couldn't stand to stare at his comatose little brother any longer. Probably a little of both. Either way, I could tell he was practically crawling out of his skin to get out of there.

Mrs. T was at the country club fulfilling her Mimosa drinking duties, so I guessed it was up to me to keep Blake entertained while he was here.

I dumped my backpack on the window seat and leaned over the bed. "Josh? Blake and I are going out for a little while. I'll talk to you later, okay?"

Blake politely said goodbye to Agatha and led the way outside.

Outside, he breathed in a lungful of air and sighed. "I don't know how you can stand it."

"It's not his fault. He's still in there somewhere, Blake. Dr. Patel says that most likely he can hear everything that's going on around him."

Blake looked skeptical and he didn't say anything else until we reached the water.

Walking down the dock with Blake felt wrong somehow. I wasn't all that nervous around Josh, so I couldn't figure out why I felt so nervous around Blake. Maybe it was because he was a slightly older, slightly more muscular version of Josh, and he had the same green eyes that seemed to pin you to the wall and gaze right into your soul.

Being around Blake made me feel like I wasn't good enough. And I never felt like that around Josh.

He was so much taller than me that I had to crane my neck to look up at him. After a while I felt silly gaping up at him with blatant admiration and wonder in my eyes that I stopped looking at him altogether and simply kept my eyes on the dock planks below my feet.

Even though he was walking slowly, his strides were a lot longer than mine and I had to practically rush to keep up with him.

Blake Thornton had been the darling of August Lake High School when he went to school here. He was captain of the football team and the apple of his parents' eyes. Then he went against their wishes and chose a college as far away as he could possibly get—Brown University in Rhode Island—and only came back to August Lake when he absolutely *had* to. He'd come back right after the accident and I had to admit I was rather surprised to find him here so soon again afterwards. Well, two and a half months might seem like a long time to me, but not to Blake.

Blake sat down next to me on the dock—a little too close for comfort, if you ask me. His arm brushed against mine and I tucked my elbow in as close to my ribs as I could without poking myself.

Blake didn't seem to mind or even notice our proximity to each other and gazed out at the water as if we hadn't touched at all. Girls—*women*—were probably comfortable with being so close to such a good-looking man, but for me it would definitely take some getting used to. He wasn't the brother I'd had my eye on for most of my life.

"You're probably wondering what I'm doing here."

He took the words right out of my mouth.

I shrugged so that he'd know he didn't have to explain himself to me. "This is your home."

He made a sound of disgust. "August Lake hasn't been my home in a long time."

For a brief moment, I wondered why it was so painfully uncomfortable for him to visit his childhood home. Josh was his *brother*. And they were only four years apart, so it wasn't like they had been complete strangers growing up.

"I'm on my way to Telluride to go camping for a few weeks before the fall semester starts."

"Colorado sounds nice." The second the words left my mouth I realized they probably made me sound like a moron.

Blake looked over at me and I averted my eyes, pretending there was something interesting happening on the tops of my sneakers.

"Have you ever been out of the state of California, Carli? There's a lot more to see than what's here in August Lake." His voice sounded bitter, but I knew it wasn't directed at me.

It wasn't like I planned on staying here forever either, but I didn't tell him about my plans for medical school. His visit wasn't about me.

August Lake wasn't just some Podunk town that was barely a speck on the map. We were barely twenty minutes away from Red Valley, which was the biggest California city north of Sacramento.

"We have a UNHL hockey team," I defended lamely. Again, I wished I'd kept my mouth shut.

"Who hasn't made it to the playoffs in who knows how long," Blake chided.

Josh didn't share his brother's narrow-minded views about August Lake. He was proud to call this town home and he looked forward to going to Red Valley State University and representing his hometown long after high school.

"My father might think August County is the only place on the map," Blake said bitterly, "but there's a whole entire world out there."

Blake had followed his own dream and had estranged his parents in the meantime. I wondered how Catherine and Warren would take the news that Josh planned on doing the same exact thing by pursuing hockey instead of finance like his dad wanted.

Part of me was jealous of Blake for venturing out and seeing the world. But the rest of me knew there was no way I could leave August Lake while Josh was in the state he was in.

What was the real reason for Blake's visit? It wasn't to tell me about his travel plans.

"I wanted to come by in person to thank you for everything you've done for my family."

Blake had come to August Lake to thank *me*?

"Oh, well, I, uh…"

He didn't seem to notice my loss for words and simply looked up at the house he'd grown up in. I followed his gaze and narrowed in on Josh's window. My vivid imagination could picture him standing there, waving to the both of us. Not wanting to be left out, he'd jog down and pester his brother to see if he had brought him a gift.

"I don't think my mom would have made it through all this without you visiting every day," Blake added.

In my opinion, Catherine was hardly making it through at all. "I don't mind," I replied. "It's the same thing I'd do if Josh were awake."

"Yeah," he said, nodding. "You two were always pretty inseparable."

A rogue wave of emotion blindsided me and I had to bite down on my tongue to keep from tearing up. I hadn't made a habit out of crying about Josh and I wasn't about to start in front of his older and wiser brother.

What was it about Blake's words that had caused tears to prick at the backs of my eyes? Because Josh and I *had* been inseparable. Not just in my eyes, but in other people's too. Our closeness wasn't something I'd built up in my head to help me cope. It was real. Just like our friendship and my feelings for him.

"Do you remember Miranda Brimley?"

Blake's voice brought me back to reality.

I did remember Miranda. She graduated in Blake's class. She had been a cheerleader, the homecoming queen...all the things I would never be (and didn't aspire to be).

"Kind of," I answered, not really sure why I was holding back.

Once again, Blake didn't seem to notice. Where Josh would have cocked his head to the side and stared me down and asked "What aren't you saying, Car?" Blake simply looked down at his feet dangling off the dock like they were the most important item in the universe.

"Miranda and I got engaged last week."

"Oh." The word slipped from my lips with such suddenness that it sounded like I disapproved. "Congratulations," I offered, trying to make a graceful recovery.

"Thanks."

"Did you tell Josh?" I watched his Adam's apple bob up and down as he swallowed.

"I'll, uh, I think I'll let you tell him for me."

"He can hear you, you know." I wanted to reassure him that his brother was still "in there," but I was afraid I only came across as condescending.

"Yeah," he said, sounding doubtful. "I was going to wait to ask her until…but…" Blake's unspoken words lingered in the air between us.

I understood. Josh wasn't showing any signs of improving and his brother shouldn't have to put his life on hold in spite of it. But I still thought Blake should have been able to tell Josh the good news himself.

I wished the Thornton's could make an effort to scrounge up a little optimism. Here I was, not even related to them, and I had a better outlook on Josh's predicament than they did. Was I being naïve and stupid? Did they know something about him that I didn't? Because the Josh I knew would be disheartened to find that his family had given up on his recovery so easily. I guess it was up to me to be optimistic for everyone. I had never been a cheerleader like Miranda Brimley, but for Josh I'd give the whole pom-pom thing a shot.

"Josh will be happy for you," I said.

"I hope so. Miranda is really great. This summer we went to…"

Blake proceeded to tell me all about their recent trip to the Bahamas and I sat and listened as if I was Josh's surrogate. I couldn't bring Blake's brother back, but I could provide a shoulder to lean on and an ear to listen.

"Miranda didn't come here with me today because I didn't really know what to expect…and I didn't want her to be…you know, put off by it."

I nodded. Seeing Josh in his current state wasn't the type of homecoming Blake had in mind for his fiancé. Not everyone was comfortable with the sight of Josh lying there motionless in bed. Not everyone could keep ahold of their emotions in a situation like this.

"Do you want to go get something to eat?" Blake asked. "You're probably cooped up in that house more than you should be."

Now he sounded like my aunt. And my dad. And everyone else I knew, for that matter.

"Thanks, but I've got to get to class."

Blake shook his head, suddenly looking amused. "Summer school was considered a bad word in the Thornton house."

I probably wouldn't be too keen about it either, but I couldn't spend every waking moment in Josh's room. Then I'd really go bonkers.

"Yeah, well, I'm trying to get a head start on college." Even though I was currently taking all the wrong classes.

"Good for you. Well, I guess this is goodbye then. I'm meeting my parents for dinner later, but I won't be back here. Not until the holidays at least."

I dreaded to think what Christmas would be like around here.

"Thanks for stopping by. It was nice to see you." Nice to be bombarded by your resemblance to Josh.

Even though Blake looked like he needed a hug, I didn't instigate one. We said our goodbyes and I went inside to retrieve my backpack.

The entire ride to school, I thought about what Blake and I would have talked about over lunch if I'd said yes.

Professor Dodd's lesson on patterns in the stock market was entirely lost on me. Instead of concentrating on microeconomics, my mind wandered off to a parallel universe where I had a sibling of my own. What would it be like to have an older brother or sister to navigate the trials of the world with? What would it be like to share my father with someone else?

Day 76

You had a visitor today. I haven't seen Blake since you were in the hospital, but he came by the house to see you this morning. He had some happy news to share with you and I hope you wake up soon to hear it. He seems really happy, Josh. Real happy.

Chapter Eleven

When I got home that evening, I had an unexpected visitor of my own. Unfortunately, she didn't look a thing like Josh. Or his brother.

"You're coming home with me." Buzzard Breath didn't even let me get all the way into the house before she declared her ultimatum.

"*What*?" After my chat with Blake and three hours of Microeconomics, Aunt Rhoda's abruptness caught me off guard.

"Gather up your things. You're coming to stay with me in Red Valley."

Uh no, I wasn't. No. Freaking. Way.

"That's not going to happen," I told her as calmly as I could manage.

Did she have *any* idea what kind of day I just had? Or how much homework I had to do? Obviously not, or she wouldn't have ambushed me, looking like a vulture standing over fresh road kill.

All I wanted to do was plop down in front of the TV and munch on some microwave popcorn before I dove into my homework. There was no time in my schedule for this kind of ridiculousness. And I wasn't willing to pencil it in either.

Shaking my head in disbelief, I shoved past her and into my room. My one place of refuge from the rest of the crazy, messed-up world.

Following me, Aunt Rhoda folded her arms over her nonexistent chest and stared me down, daring me to blink.

I blinked all right, as well as forcibly shook my head like a crazy person being pushed too far. "I'm not going anywhere with you."

"I'll report your situation to Child Services," she threatened.

"So?" I spat. Instead of sounding calm and grownup, I sounded like the bratty teenager she thought I was. Emotions really had a way of screwing up a situation.

"Then your dad will be in *big trouble*." Her tone sounded like it was directed at a four-year-old, but the message was clear.

I would die before I let harm—physical or state-mandated—come to my dad.

"You *wouldn't*," I challenged.

"I would. When they hear that a sixteen-year-old is living by herself—"

"I'm not living alone. My dad will be back soon and I'm almost seventeen."

"Doesn't matter. You're underage."

"Stay for how long?" She might be dishing out threats, but I wasn't above bargaining for my freedom.

"Until your father gets back."

That could be weeks—he'd gone on another run to Southern California and who knows where after that—but I'd figure something out by then.

For years, because of Dad's job, I had felt like a grown up. I took care of things around the house and was generally in charge of my own destiny by default. Now, Aunt Rhoda was looking down at me like she alone held all the power in her bony fingers and I was stripped of all rights.

The words hurt to say out loud, but I was left with no other choice. With no father figure to help bail me out, I'd been backed into a corner. "Okay."

Aunt Rhoda gave a sharp nod and told me to gather up my things. "Give me your phone," she ordered through clenched teeth.

"No way. I'm calling my dad."

"He already knows what's going on."

Did that mean he had approved it? Or was Rhoda a concerned citizen gone rogue?

"Give it here or else you're only going to make things worse for yourself."

I couldn't lose my only link to Josh, but dealing with Aunt Rhoda was like trying to reason with Josh when he was hungry. It wasn't worth it.

Handing my phone over to Rhoda the Terrible felt like I was giving her one of my limbs. Somehow I'd find a way to make things right again. I was smart—in the top of my class—and I wasn't going to let this bulldog of a woman stand between me and what mattered most in my life.

"Now go pack a suitcase."

Moving at the speed of three-toed sloth, I did as she ordered. Under protest. Reluctantly. Grudgingly. Mrs. Reed would be proud.

Standing in my room, I looked around at the four walls and everything within them. How in the world was I supposed to simply pack up all of my belongings and "move" to Red Valley for an indeterminate amount of time? I had a lifetime of memories in this room and about three minutes to throw together a suitcase. I knew I wouldn't be leaving it forever, but this had been the only room I knew. Dad had let me change the paint colors over the years. Dad had built the bookcase for me. Dad had helped me pick out the lavender bedding, despite claims that he knew nothing about "girly stuff."

In the end, I fit a few outfits into the weekender bag Dad had bought me for eighth grade graduation—"for all the adventures you're going to go on"—and added my toiletries from the bathroom. This sure wasn't what I'd had in mind when I thought about my future "adventures."

After making sure I had all the books and papers I needed, I grabbed my backpack and slung it over my shoulder and met Aunt Rhoda outside by her car.

My hands were shaking I was so angry. How could she do this to me? How could she do this to *my dad*? *Her brother*?

Family really wasn't all it was cracked up to be.

Josh was more like family to me than this horrible hag of a woman. How was it possible that we were even related? Dad had some explaining to do about the ole family tree.

After Aunt Rhoda practically shoved me into her car, we headed south. And I grinded my teeth together as her little car bumped along the road.

I had a potted plant of my own, a little succulent that my dad had bought me—and I didn't even get a chance to take it to Josh's where the nurses could keep it watered for me. (I refused to bring it with me because that meant I had resigned to moving in with Rhoda. Which I most definitely HAD NOT.)

At the first stoplight we came to I wanted to throw the passenger side door open and run like a banshee back toward home. But I was being blackmailed. And you can't protect yourself when someone has that kind of power over you.

The real icing on the cake was when Rhoda tried to make small talk with me about the weather during the ride to her house.

I was not having it.

"Do you mind if we ride in silence?" I asked in a sickly-sweet voice. "I kind of have a lot on my mind right now." To me, it sounded like a perfectly reasonable request and I guess Aunt Rhoda agreed, because she turned up the radio and didn't say another word until we reached her apartment—apartment?!—in Red Valley.

Oh, she had some nerve! She had commandeered me, plucked me unwillingly from my cozy little house, uprooted me, to bring me to a one-bedroom *apartment*.

My mouth hung open when she led me inside and I didn't care if she thought it was rude. The place was the size of a shoebox, or more aptly a Cracker Jack box. But there was no prize within these four walls. No prize at all.

No wonder she'd never invited us over before. Between the tiny living room and the itty-bitty galley kitchen, there was absolutely nowhere to entertain company.

"I'll make the sofa bed up for you after dinner."

Sofa bed? I looked over at the couch that had seen better days and glared at it. High and Mighty Aunt Rhoda had stormed my little castle and didn't even have anything to offer me besides a *sofa bed*?

Now I wanted her to contact Child Services just so I could give them a strongly worded letter written by yours truly. The headline would read "Grief-stricken Child Torn from Home and Forced to Sleep on Sofa Bed."

All in a matter of an hour, my home, dignity, and privacy had been stripped from me. All in one fell swoop, as Mrs. Reed always said. I forget exactly what the words meant, but I could certainly relate. It felt like I was both falling and swooping at the same time.

I made a vow to myself right then and there. No matter if it took me all night, I would come up with a plan to get out of this. My freedom and sanity depended on it. Surely my dad would understand. But if they took me away from him, one way or another, I would still be up the creek without a paddle.

Happy rowing, Carli.

That night, I waited until Aunt Rhoda went to bed before I took out my notebook. There was no way in Hades I was going to let her get her grubby little hands on my most personal, private thoughts and feelings.

Rhoda's Red Valley Prison

Day One

Today might be one for the record books. First, I was blackmailed by my own auntie dearest and then kidnapped to be held at a secure location in Red Valley until further notice.

As long as she keeps me here I won't be able to update you about your condition. But, Josh, please know that I will do everything short of burning down the city to get back to you again. Just rest easy knowing that you are in good hands with Agatha and Mamie. Dr. Patel will be by for his regular visit tomorrow. He knows what he's talking about, so be sure to listen to everything he says.

The guard has gone to sleep and I can report that she snores like a lumberjack sawing logs in a Pacific Northwest forest. Dinner might as well have been bread and water because said guard is highly deficient in the cooking department. Chicken was rubbery, rice was undercooked, and vegetables would have been snubbed by the most ravenous of rabbits.

Dang it! I smacked my palm against my forehead—quietly, as not to wake the sentinel. I forgot to pack my Pop-Tarts! They should have been the first thing I grabbed on my way out of the house. There was no telling what kind of cardboard-flavored cereal Rhoda kept stocked in her teeny tiny pantry.

To make matters worse—oh, yes, things could always get worse—she didn't have a spare pillow to give me and expected me to use a decorative throw pillow from the couch. Which might not have been so bad if it didn't have annoying little sequins sewn all over it. I was seriously rethinking my decision to not put up a bigger fight before coming here.

And then there was the matter of my classes. I had another day before missing class would become an issue, but I had a feeling Aunt Rhoda didn't share my commitment to advanced education. Maybe she'd drive me to class all the way back in August Lake just to get rid of me for a few hours. Maybe not.

Probably not.

I don't think she realized just how complicated it would be to uproot a teenager and plop them (me) down into a foreign environment and expect them (me) to thrive. I was a delicate plant that had been repotted and by the end of this battle-of-the-wills, I had a feeling I was going to go without essentials like water and sunshine. Ah, but the fertilizer was being dumped on me in droves.

Oh, how I wanted to slip out the door and into the night and run back to my beloved August Lake! But I couldn't do that to my dad. The consequences of that tiny sliver of freedom would cost too much and linger much too long.

P.S.

I never thought I'd ask you this, Josh, but could you maybe wait to wake up until I come back to August Lake? Okay, thanks.

Your sequestered, soon to be on-the-lam best friend,

Carlina Gabriella Thornley

I signed the entry with a flourish, my best version of a movie star signature. The same one Josh and I had practiced in eighth grade for when we both became famous and had to sign endless autographs for adoring fans.

Leaning back on my sequin pillow, I tried to remain calm.

The kitchen faucet dripped and Rhoda's fridge was making all sorts of hissing and banging noises. The clock in the kitchen ticked in time with the ceiling fan rotating above me. I could hear the next-door neighbors scraping chairs across the linoleum and then a toilet flushed. Then I heard footsteps above, up on the second floor. Were these the kinds of noises Josh heard while he was laying there in his hospital bed? Could he really hear what was going on around him? Or was that just a ploy the doctors and nurses used to give us hope? Someday I would get the opportunity to ask him.

While the appliances transmitted sweet nothings to one another and the neighbors went about their noisy nightly activities, I sat cross-legged on the sofa bed and thought about what I was missing out on in August Lake. I knew I would be able to return—eventually—but I hadn't been ready to leave. I didn't know what kind of game Rhoda was playing or why she'd pulled the power move on me, but I wouldn't let her win. I had a dad and a house and a best friend who needed me. And I couldn't help anyone from a sofa bed.

Sitting in the dark, completely cut off from the world, was an unsettling thing. Without Josh and Agatha and Gordie, I felt so alone. I *was* alone. The person in the next room didn't care about me. Gordie would think that I abandoned him and Josh. He wouldn't understand my awful human problems.

A helicopter circled overhead and I let myself imagine that there was a search party out looking for me. Round and round, the helicopter scanned the neighborhood, before finally moving on and leaving the apartment silent. Except for the hibernating bear sounds coming from the bedroom, of course. Man, that lady could saw logs!

Laughter bubbled up inside my chest and I had to cover my mouth with my hand to keep from busting up.

It was official. I had gone completely and irrevocably insane.

And it felt absolutely liberating.

Chapter Twelve

The next morning, I woke up to the sound of the earth rumbling. At first, I thought we were having an earthquake. But then I realized it was just a diesel truck idling outside.

A diesel truck?

Wondering if my bout of insanity last night was permanent, I hopped up onto my knees. The lumpy sofa bed protested beneath my weight and I scooted over to the window and peeked through the metal mini-blinds.

My bruised spirit soared. Even the tips of my hair were happy. The cavalry had arrived in the form of a Kenworth truck.

Dad's Timberland work boots ate up the concrete path to the apartment, the flannel shirt he was wearing fluttering along in his wake. Dark denim covered his thick, tree trunk legs and worn cotton stretched across his barrel-like chest. His face was grim, set with creasing lines around his mouth and across his forehead. Carl Thornley was a man on a mission.

And soon Aunt Rhoda would be road kill.

Dad's meaty fist banged on the door, no doubt rattling the entire apartment complex.

As much as I wanted to run to the door, swing it open and fling myself into his arms, I held back and sat back away from the blinds. I remained in my spot on the sofa bed and watched as Aunt Rhoda padded in from the bedroom, tugging her robe tightly around her. The creases on her face matched my dad's. Under different circumstances, I would have burst out laughing at the alarmed and worried look on her face. But now was not the time to show amusement.

Aunt Rhoda looked through the peephole, mumbled something under her breath, and slowly opened the door. I pulled my knees up to my chest, settled in and prepared to be entertained. This was going to be good.

"What in the *hell* is going on?" my dad's voice roared.

In all of my sixteen—almost seventeen—years, I don't think I've ever heard him sound so angry. And that's counting the time I accidently bleached his favorite pair of black jeans.

Without waiting for an answer, he pushed past his trembling half-sister and looked around the room, his eyes finally settling on me. I gave him a feeble wave from my spot on my new sofa bed and sent him a sort of I-told-you-so half smile.

"Get your stuff," he said gruffly in my general direction.

In a state of amusement/shock/relief, I swung onto the floor and grabbed my belongings.

Then my dad turned his attention to Aunt Rhoda.

Towering over her, he crossed his arms over his chest and glared. "You leave a threatening, cryptic message on my phone and then kidnap my daughter?"

"I did not *kidnap* her." Aunt Rhoda's voice was weak and shaking, just like her knobby knees.

Dad ignored her. "I drove all night to get here and I'm not in the mood for games. I was all the way in Bakersfield."

On my way out the door, I stopped in front of Aunt Rhoda and put my hand out. "My phone?"

She stared at me, not wanting to give an inch. Finally, after a grunt from my dad, she let out a frustrated sigh and went to get her purse. She yanked the phone out and thrust it at me like it was the devil incarnate.

Shouldering my backpack, I followed my dad outside. I didn't look down, but I was sure there was smoke coming from my Converse in my haste to get the heck out of there. It might have all been a blur, but I was leaving this sofa bed nightmare and that was all that mattered.

I hadn't showered yet—oh! how I had been looking forward to discovering what pleasantries the tiny stall shower held!—but my hygiene was the last thing on my mind. It was like I'd been paroled—what exactly had I done wrong again?—and was being freed on good behavior. I knew a lifetime of please and thank-you's would come back and reward me someday.

The whole experience had left me feeling a little raw around the edges and a lot sarcastic. In the morning, when I woke up in my own bed, in my very own bedroom, everything would look a little better. I was sure of it.

In the two seconds it took for us to storm outside, Aunt Rhoda must have gathered up some courage because she stomped out after us, looking like a Chihuahua ready to take on a Rottweiler. In fact, she rushed after us like we were taking off with her jewelry and valuables or something.

"Thorn!" She sounded more like his mother than his sister and I found it hard to believe that there was actually someone out in the world who had the guts to talk down to my dad like that. This was no puny accounts payable clerk. This was a man who'd make Bull Hurley in *Over the Top* tremble in his steel-toe boots. (When I was little, I watched *Smokey and the Bandit* and *Over the Top* a half million times. Somehow those old movies about truck drivers made me feel a little closer to my dad when he was on the road.)

Although I had plenty to say to Aunt Rhoda, especially now that I knew there wouldn't be any consequences, I didn't stop to add my two cents worth. I simply climbed up into the safety of the truck and waited for my rescue to be complete.

With her beaky nose tilted up to the sky, Aunt Rhoda continued to yell at my dad's back like he was a speck on the pavement. "She needs a stable home with parental supervision!"

Dad wheeled around and I thought I felt the earth move beneath the truck. "*This* isn't her home," he spat, nodding to the shabby apartment complex. "And what do you know about how to raise a child?"

"I…I…" Aunt Rhoda sputtered, trying to find some words to defend herself.

Dad was like a shark and he had already sensed blood in the water. "You just want to call yourself a guardian and get your grubby little hands on some cool social security checks, don't you? You thought an easy way to get out of your own craphole of a life would be to wheedle your way in, take advantage of me, and kidnap my daughter. Now you stay away from her and I mean it. If you *ever* try another stunt like that again, I'll…"

I watched him swallow down the threat on her life. Then he balled up his fists, relaxed them, and clenched them again. "You'll stay the hell away from us if you know what's best for you."

Dad swung up into the truck, started it and the faithful truck rumbled to life. He waited for an opening in traffic and then we lurched out onto the road. Heading north had never felt so good.

"You okay?" he asked without looking over at me.

"Yeah." I swallowed. Fear and excitement sure made my throat dry. "She blindsided me yesterday. I tried to call you, but—"

"Yeah, I know. You won't ever have to worry about her again."

"Thanks, Dad." I'd never forget the image of him reverberating anger and glowing like a hero.

At the next stoplight he reached over and squeezed my shoulder. His jaw was working like he was still having a silent argument with his "well-meaning" sister.

"I'm okay," I said, reminding myself it was over.

"I love you, Lina, and there's nothin' I wouldn't do for you."

Dad. My rescuer. My hero.

My heart felt like it might burst through my ribcage, like it had grown a few sizes. Kind of like the Grinch who stole Christmas. I'd spent all summer making sacrifices for Josh and now my own dad was returning the favor.

As my dad pulled onto the freeway, I turned my phone on. With what battery life was left, I checked my messages. Other than an "all is well" text from Agatha at the end of her shift last night, the coast was clear.

What a relief! I was sure I'd missed out on some pivotal part of Josh's recovery, but all was well.

His vitals are good.

When we got home, the first thing I wanted to do was rush over to Josh's. But I quickly reminded myself that if none of that fiasco had happened last night, I wouldn't have gone over to his house for at least another hour anyway. There would be a lot to discuss with my dad. Now that I knew I wouldn't be restricted from seeing him again, Josh could wait a little while longer.

"We've got some things to talk about."

I had just dropped my things onto my bed—my real bed with a real mattress—and Dad stood in my doorway with his arms folded. He didn't look mean or spitting-nails angry. He just looked concerned. And a little worried.

"I'm fine, Dad," I reassured him and plunked down on my bed. Thank goodness for a real memory foam pillow. I would sleep like a baby tonight.

"Are you really okay?"

My dad knew me well. Even if something was terribly wrong, he knew I'd sugarcoat it just to spare him the headache.

"Yeah." I finger-combed my bed-head hair. I hoped this discussion didn't take long because I really needed to take a shower and get over to see Josh. "She took my phone away and I had no way to check on Josh and that really freaked me out, but other than that…I'm okay."

"You can go over later and see him. After your chores are done."

That made me smile. "Of course."

"But what about next time?" he asked.

"I don't think she's going to try anything again," I assured him.

"I mean the next time you need me and I'm out of town. I hauled ass to get to you, but—"

"*Dad*," I said sternly. "It's okay. I'm going to be fine."

I had needed him. And for the first time in a long time he was there.

"Leaving you alone was the wrong thing to do. After your mom…and after the accident, I ran. I shouldn't have left you. I guess it was how I dealt with everything that happened."

"It's okay, Dad. Everyone does something to deal with life. Mrs. T drinks too much. That's how she deals with Josh's…situation. And Mr. T works eighteen hours a day. And I escape into my schoolwork and books. It's okay," I repeated.

"No, it's not. I shoulda been there for you. Instead I wanted to pawn you off onto your Aunt Rhoda."

"Really, Dad, it's okay," I insisted.

"No, it's not. I've been a terrible father to leave my teenage daughter all by herself. I've had a lot of time to think on the road. It's pretty much all there *is* to do. And I've decided to only take local runs from now on. I've got a year with you before you go off to college and then you're going to start a life of your own. There's plenty of time to chase those white dotted lines after you graduate."

The more I thought about it, the more I liked the sound of my dad being home more often.

"I'd like that. We could have dinner together more often and actually do stuff. Like going to the movies."

"Yeah," Dad agreed. "It's time I start spending more time with my best girl."

Day 78

Today was my birthday. I brought a cake over to your house. (You should've seen me carry it over on the handlebars on my bike!)

Gordie barked at the lit candles and Agatha and I had to blow them out real fast so he'd stop going ballistic.

The cake was delicious. It had that extra sugary icing that makes your teeth feel like they're going to fall out after you eat it. You would have loved it.

I was hoping you'd wake up in time to celebrate with me, but I guess that wasn't in the cards.

I still have the locket you gave me for my birthday last year.

The memory of that day remained fresh in my mind.

"I thought you could put a picture of your mom inside," Josh had said, sounding hopeful.

"I will," I had told him. I'd put a picture of Josh inside the locket, too. "I love it."

I had to reign in my excitement that day. There was no way I was going to give Josh any reason to regret the beautiful and thoughtful gift.

I have a picture of you inside the locket, along with one of my mom. It's nice to have something special to wear close to my heart.

You seemed embarrassed when you gave it to me, like it was too intimate a gift for someone who was just a friend. I'm not embarrassed to wear it, Josh.

Anyway, later my dad took me out to dinner and we had a really nice time. He said he's going to start spending more time at home and I'm looking forward to him being around more. He even offered to teach me how to drive! Which brings me to my birthday surprise...

You'll never guess what Dad bought me for my birthday!

A car! Well, it's technically an SUV. It's a Jeep Cherokee. It's used, but I prefer the term "pre-owned." Dad said he wanted me to have something to take my driver's test in. I've been studying like crazy and I think I I'm going to ace it. After all, I was the one who quizzed you when you were getting ready to take yours. I hope I pass it on the first try like you did.

The Jeep is an automatic—which is a relief that I don't have to learn how to drive a stick-shift right away. Dad had Gus check it out before he bought it because he's the best mechanic in the North State and

Dad trusts him. I think he's as nervous about me driving as I am.

I know I've been putting off taking the test, but the more I think about it, the more I know I'm going to love the freedom of hopping in a car and going wherever I want.

As soon as you wake up, I'll take you for a ride to wherever you want to go.

Later that morning, my dad took me to the DMV to get my provisional permit. Then we'd take the Jeep out for my first driving lesson. It was time I learned. Besides, it probably looked strange for the daughter of a truck driver to not have a driver's license.

Yep, it was time for me to put on my big-girl pants and stare adulthood in the face.

Chapter Thirteen

Regaining consciousness is not instant. In the first few days, coma patients are only awake for a few minutes and that duration of time gradually increases. Many awake in a profound state of confusion, not knowing how they got there and sometimes suffering from the inability to articulate any speech. That's what I read anyway.

And that's exactly how it happened with Josh.

Everything happened so fast. One minute Josh was asleep like he'd been for the past three months, and the next his eyes were open and he was looking around like he didn't know where he was.

I couldn't believe my own eyes. Josh was awake!

"Josh!" I flew over to his bed from the window seat where I had been writing and leaned over him. "Josh?" My breathing sped up and I sucked in short, shallow breaths. "Can you hear me?" I laced my fingers through his. "Squeeze my hand if you can hear me."

Without moving his head, he blinked and looked out at the room again, avoiding my gaze.

Josh, are you in there? Please let the answer be yes.

Not that long ago, Josh would have sprung out of bed, pulled on some clothes and ran out the door in search of an adventure. Now, he just laid there as still as a corpse, and scanned the room with disinterested eyes. Where was the spark that had inhabited those green eyes ever since the first moment they'd looked at me? Where was the energy, the fire that had coursed through his veins?

Gone. Or at least dormant for the time being.

"Okay. How 'bout this," I suggested. "If you can't squeeze my hand, then blink again if you can hear me."

Slowly, as if the movement drained away every ounce of energy he had, Josh closed his eyes. As I waited with bated breath for him to blink them open again, my mind raced. All he had to do was open them again and we'd have shared our first connection, our first communication, in months.

"I'm calling Dr. Patel." Agatha's voice was like a fly buzzing in the background.

"Josh, it's me. Carli. I've been with you the whole time. Can you open your eyes and look at me again?"

But Josh didn't open his eyes again. He went back to sleep without acknowledging my request. Back to that place that had such a hold on him.

It didn't matter. He had blinked two times in a row and his eyes had moved back and forth as if he'd been looking at his surroundings. That was more progress than he'd shown in months.

Progress. Josh was finally making progress.

Had he seen me?

The blank way he'd looked at me answered the question for me.

"Dr. Patel said he's ten minutes away," Agatha told me.

Ten minutes probably meant at least thirty. How come there was never a doctor around when you needed one?

I paced back and forth across the room so many times that Agatha finally put her hand out to stop me. "Give Josh, child," she reminded me.

Hadn't I given enough? How much longer did I have to wait for him? Until I was old and wrinkled and too senile to remember what I was waiting for?

After waiting several more hours, Josh continued to sleep. He slept through Dr. Patel's examination and he slept through Catherine returning home and passing out on the chaise lounge on the sun porch.

"You really should go home and get some sleep." Agatha's voice was motherly yet commanding.

"But I don't want to miss out on anything." This was what I'd been waiting for and now I might miss out on it all because the human body required sleep. *Real* sleep. The kind you woke up after eight hours of.

Agatha looked up from her knitting and leveled me with a look she'd probably used on her own children a time or two. "I know you don't, hon, but you're no good to anyone if you're delirious with sleep deprivation."

She was right. It was tough to admit, but she was right.

Leaving Josh felt like the wrong thing to do. But, unfortunately, I could barely keep my eyes open.

There was always tomorrow.

"Will you call me if anything happens...if he wakes up again?"

"You know I will."

"All right."

Day 87

Why won't you wake up again? It's been two days, Josh, and I'm sick and tired of waiting for you to

I flung my pen across the room and it bounced off my desk and landed on the carpet. Now I was beginning to sound whiny and desperate and that wasn't the journal's purpose.

What was its purpose? To keep me sane while Josh took his sweet time getting around to opening his eyes again?

Huffing, I got up, retrieved the pen and sat back down on my bed with the journal splayed across my lap. The first thing I did was scribble out my last entry and then I slammed the journal shut and went outside for some fresh air.

That night, sleep was impossible, but I lay in my bed and tried for it anyway. When you wanted something so badly your heart ached with it, it was best to ignore it and let it come to you. At least that's what I was trying to do.

My mind wandered around, up, down, back and forth, in a pathetic attempt to make sense of the situation. Slowly but surely Josh was trying to make his way back to us. And instead of being there with him, I was on the other side of town, cursing the nonexistent lumps in my mattress.

Maybe we were both dead or in limbo. Maybe Josh had gone toward the white light and I had stayed behind. Was I destined to haunt him forever?

Nighttime used to be the worst. I would toss and turn in bed, my mind frantically analyzing every last detail of the accident and trying to make sense of it. When you're trying to fall asleep, it really doesn't help to have an active imagination conjuring up things you have no right thinking about.

Now, I tried to clear my head, reassure myself that my phone was nearby in case of emergency and know that I would pick up life where I left off the very next day. For the most part, it worked. And then there were nights like tonight when no matter how tired I was and how much I tried, sleep just won't come…

I can still hear the sound of the metal twisting and screaming all around us. When I reach out to Josh, my hand is met with carbon fiber instead of skin. Everything is cold, the steel jagged and rough against the skin on my fingertips.

On the driver's side of the car, where Josh is supposed to be, the dashboard is mangled into an unnatural shape. The steering wheel isn't in the right place either and the rearview mirror is nowhere to be seen. It all looks like some kind of weird dream where the images are distorted like they're being seen in a funhouse mirror.

I can't see around the airbag and it threatens to suffocate me as it presses hard against my face and chest.

"Josh?"

I know he's there, right next to me, but I can't hear him and he doesn't answer me.

Why won't he answer me?

"*Josh?*" I try again, but my mouth is so dry that it hurts to speak. When I try to swallow, I immediately taste copper.

Blood.

As if things can't get any worse. I am bleeding and Josh won't answer me.

We are supposed to be going to a baseball game, but it feels like we aren't anywhere at all. We are in limbo, encased in a prison of unforgiving steel and shattered glass.

The seatbelt is trying its hardest to choke me. Nothing is where it should be. The center console has folded like an accordion and the dashboard appears to be nonexistent. No, it was just in my lap, that's all.

I want to pinch myself so that I can wake up where everything is normal, but it isn't necessary. My legs and feet are already being pinched within an inch of their life. That means I am already awake. That meant this isn't a nightmare and is actually happening to us.

Every breath I try to suck into my lungs burns like it doesn't belong there. I can smell gasoline and my own fear.

Wherever we are, I knew we aren't supposed to be here. And where was Josh when I needed him? Why wasn't he answering me when just a second ago he was seated right beside me and we were—

Well, now I couldn't quite remember what we'd been doing or where we'd been going. Whatever it was, this wasn't it. This wasn't where we belonged.

Josh liked to play pranks and joke around, but this wasn't some elaborate prank of his. This was much too bizarre to be real. Josh didn't do things to hurt people. To pinch their legs and constrict their lungs. As fuzzy as my head was, I knew this wasn't his doing.

Who had done this to us? Why would someone hurt Josh and leave me all alone like this?

It takes an agonizingly long time for help to arrive. I can hear voices all around the car, but none of them belong to Josh. His is the only voice I'm listening for and I don't answer when an older man's disembodied voice asks if I'm all right.

I'm not all right and Josh still isn't answering me.

Where is he?

Sirens sound different when you know they're coming for you. When you're at home and you hear a siren, you know that something bad has happened and that they're rushing to or from something traumatic. When you hear them coming toward you, and you know that help is coming, it's difficult to keep your eyes open…

There are more voices. Someone shines a bright light into my eyes and it feels like they are driving a spike through my head. Parts of me are numb and other parts—important parts like my head and chest—hurt more than I ever thought possible. Breathing is difficult, but I keep doing it because I need to see Josh.

They—the voices—are shouting out garbled words and numbers and I can hear the crunch of glass as someone walks over it with heavy footfalls. When I try to crane my head to look for Josh, my neck won't cooperate because it has been secured in a brace. They have strapped my whole body down and I can't move at all.

Up I go onto the gurney and into the ambulance. When I look over my toes all I can see is Josh's car, mangled and unrecognizable on the bridge.

"Josh?" My lips aren't working properly and it's impossible to be heard over all the chaos. So many people are talking around me and a saw screeches in the distance.

They put something over my mouth to help me breathe. An oxygen mask.

"Jawwsh."

And then my head stops hurting so much and I begin to feel blissfully numb all over.

"Jaww…"

Chapter Fourteen

When my phone rang the next morning, it woke me up from a tormented sleep. Dreams would have been welcomed, but instead of indulging in surreal images, my brain relived the accident over and over from every different angle until I woke up screaming in the middle of the night. Sometime around four a.m. I drifted off to sleep again, exhausted and terror-stricken.

"Carli…it's Josh…" The urgency in Agatha's voice froze me in place, rooted my feet to the floor and made my stomach drop down into my shoes.

This was the call I had been dreading for months. I hadn't prepared myself for it because how could you ready yourself for such a thing?

But I had skipped ahead and imagined Josh's funeral. It was a terrible thing to do, but I had done it all the same. His mother dressed in black from head to toe, his father in a designer suit, his crisp white shirt in stark contrast to his black jacket and slacks. Blake would be there, looking much too handsome for such a sad day. He'd be wearing black, too. And his face would be strained with an expression of grief mixed in with disbelief.

How could this have happened? he'd ask himself.

Miranda would squeeze Blake's hand from her place beside him and he'd look over at her sympathetic face and wonder how he was supposed to get over losing his only brother. Miranda would do and say all the right things to comfort her fiancé. And Blake would take comfort in knowing he had a shoulder to cry on in his time of need.

I'd make sure to stand next to Agatha because she'd be the only one who'd understand if I collapsed. And My father would have the physical strength to pick me back up again.

The only reason Josh had died was because I had been weak enough to let the image of his funeral form in my mind. I had willed it all to come true because I'd cracked under the pressure.

This was all my fault.

When he'd opened his eyes the other day, it was his way of saying goodbye.

Goodbye, Josh.

I will still love you until forever.

"He's asking for you." Agatha's voice ripped me out of the scenario I'd fabricated and back into the present.

Twelve different trains of thought collided inside my brain. And suddenly everything grinded to a halt. Josh was alive and he was asking for me. My worst nightmare hadn't become a reality. There was still time to save him.

"He's talking?" I asked in disbelief. Maybe I *was* dreaming.

"Yes." Agatha's voice was watery. "And he's asking to see you."

The image in my mind shifted. The funeral, the horrible black funeral, blurred and then a new image became clear. Now I could see Josh at a hockey game, jumping to his feet, cheering on his favorite team with his fists in the air. And then he was on the boat dock, throwing a stick out into the water while Gordie shot off like a bullet to retrieve it. Without waiting for Gordie to swim all the way back, Josh did a cannonball into the water, spraying half the dock with water in the process. A second later, he surfaced, his head bobbing above the rippling water. He was smiling, frantically waving his arms at me, begging me to join him. He was smiling.

He was very much alive. And he was asking for me.

"I'll be right there."

When I arrived, Josh's mom was already in the room. Dr. Patel was there, too. And Agatha was wearing the biggest smile I'd ever seen her smile.

Here we were. Josh's little support group. Beside him through thick and thin.

The only person missing was Warren. The last I heard, Josh's dad was in Boston on one of his infamous business trips.

I sat my backpack by the door and slowly made my way into the room, past Josh's fan club.

It was as if he'd waited for an audience. That was so like Josh.

When I looked at Josh, everyone else faded into the background. Our eyes met and Josh's eyes flickered in recognition.

And then he smiled at me. It was a little lopsided, like the left side of his face couldn't quite make the moment, but he smiled nonetheless. "Hey…Carlina…Thornley."

"Hi, Joshua."

Everything inside me jumped for joy. And yet, somehow I stood there, calm and still, so as not to alarm Josh.

He had woken up again.

And he knew who I was!

I hadn't reminded him of my name today. He'd remembered it all on his own!

This was all too good to be true.

My heart wanted to jump out of my chest and do the Macarena or bust out some "Gangnam Style" moves at the foot of his bed. I wanted to scream at the top of my lungs and hear my voice echo past the tips of the pine trees beyond his house. Josh was awake!!!

Finally. *Josh was awake.*

All vitals are good and Josh was finally awake.

Mrs. T pulled me in for a bone-crushing hug. Her eyes were rimmed with red and this time it wasn't from alcohol. She abruptly let me go and leaned over her son.

"Josh, it's your mom again. Can you hear me, baby?" She lightly tapped his cheek with her open palm.

There was no recognition in his eyes. He looked at her blankly and then back to me.

"Do you know your name?" Dr. Patel asked him even though I'd just said it to him.

Josh looked so confused. So helpless and afraid.

He couldn't answer the question.

Josh licked his lips. "Thirsty."

Everyone looked around frantically for water. I hurried over to the water bottle on the desk and poured some into a glass. Agatha plopped a straw into the glass and Catherine snatched it out of my hand to rush over to Josh. On the way back to the bed, she tripped over Gordie and the water went flying. "Somebody get *that dog* out of here!" she screeched.

Gordie's ears flickered at the sound and he was oblivious that he was the cause of it.

Josh clicked his fingers—or he tried to anyway—and Gordie jumped up on the bed. Ever so carefully, Gordie walked up beside Josh's legs as if he knew Josh was fragile and then finally settled beside his waist.

Josh's lips twitched, like he was trying to smile. "How…long…?" He struggled to find his words. It was like his vocabulary was a step behind his body and hadn't woken up yet.

"Oh, it doesn't matter now, honey," his mom told him, waving his question away. She was laughing and crying at the same time.

"Car?" he asked.

His voice was so scratchy and hoarse that it sounded like it was painful to speak.

"Your car is fine," Catherine reassured him.

I frowned, not knowing why his mom felt the need to lie to protect him.

"Car?" he asked again.

"I'm here, Josh. I'm right here."

He reached for my hand and then let it drop back down on the bed. He was too weak to lift his own hand.

Just then, Warren rushed in, looking like he'd sprinted through six counties in his three-piece suit to get here. "Is it true? I came as fast as I could." He shouldered his way past Catherine and looked down at his son.

"Dad?"

Warren swallowed hard, blinking back tears. "Son. You're awake."

Josh blinked slowly and then his eyes closed. And then he fell back to sleep.

"Is it okay for him to go to sleep?" Catherine asked Dr. Patel. "I don't want to lose him again. I can't lose him again, Doctor."

I, too, was afraid that Josh would slip back into the coma as soon as he fell asleep. Would that even happen? Hadn't he slept enough?

Dr. Patel reassured us that Josh still had a long road of recovery ahead of him and that he still had a lot of rest to catch up on—as crazy as it sounded—and that it was perfectly okay to let Josh set his own pace.

For the last three months his brain couldn't even stay awake, so I wasn't the least bit surprised.

I didn't want to go home. Josh was finally awake—for real this time, speaking and everything—and it was all I could do to tear myself away. I wanted to curl up at the foot of his bed like Gordie and never leave. I wanted Josh to talk to me. To *really* talk to me. I wanted to hear his voice say my name again. I wanted everything to be back to the way it was, back before he had a skeleton for a body and a loss for words.

But I had waited this long. I could wait longer. I could wait as long as it took for him to get back to normal again. Patience was something I'd learned I had a surplus of. There was no other way to explain how I had made it through the last twelve weeks. And now my exercise in superhuman patience had finally paid off.

I couldn't convince Gordie to leave the room, so I ordered him to stay where he was on the bed and stay out of trouble. Now that his master had shown signs of life, there was no way Gordie was losing sight of him. I couldn't blame him.

"I'll be back in the morning, Josh. Wake up again for me tomorrow, okay?"

I squeezed his hand one more time before I left. My body might be on the way back home, but my mind would stay here with him all night.

I looked back. "Be a good boy," I warned Gordie.

Gordie shifted his paws and licked Josh's hand. The dog reveled in the attention. He was as happy as a clam. Now that Josh was awake, all was right in his little doggie world.

As for me, now that Josh was awake, my world was as topsy-turvy as ever. Josh woke up not knowing who his mother was. How heartbreaking was it to have your son look at you like he'd never seen you before? I couldn't imagine how Catherine must feel right now.

As Josh slept, Warren put his arm around Catherine and pulled her close. It was the first time I'd seen him offer her comfort.

My throat constricted and I fled from the room before my tears could make a fool of me. I slipped outside and let the family reunion continue in private.

Warren, who had made himself scarce throughout most of Josh's coma, was stepping back into his role as husband and father. He wasn't running from his family anymore. And they had welcomed him with open arms.

Where was my shoulder to cry on? Nothing made sense. Everything was confusing. It felt like a dream. Josh was awake, but everything was a far cry from what it used to be.

I went outside and looked at the same view I'd been staring at for months. The water lapped at the shore, spreading and retreating. *Moving.* A hawk soared overhead, scanning for prey. *Hunting* and *flying*. Tall pines swayed in the breeze. *Growing* and *reacting* to their environment. Even though the scenery was the same, it all looked different to me. Clearer. More vivid. More *alive*.

Then why did I still feel so sad and broken inside?

Then it hit me. I did have someone to run to. I did have a shoulder to cry on.

Hopping onto my bike, I reveled in the knowledge that I, too, had someone who had the ability to comfort me.

Ten minutes later, I found my dad tinkering in the garage. Not bothering to lower the kickstand, I let my bike fall onto the driveway and he whipped around when he heard the clatter of my pedals hitting the concrete.

When he saw my face, he strode toward me, putting his hands on my arms to steady me.

"Hey, Dad." My voice waivered. I held my breath, but a sob escaped anyway.

"What happened?" Concern etched the wrinkles on his face, the same masculine face I'd been looking to for guidance since I was a little girl who felt lost without her mother. As much as he'd tried to step in and fulfill the role of both mother and father, it was an impossible task. But he'd tried anyway. And, up until the accident, it had been enough. And then he'd ran, much in the same way Warren had. But now he was here, puttering around in the garage, looking at me like he was willing to take on the world on my behalf.

Strong arms came around me, holding me together as I cried. After months of feeling completely alone, I finally let loose the emotions I'd dammed up. I finally had a shoulder to cry on.

I was a fraud. These last few months I had merely been pretending to be strong. In reality, I was absolutely terrified of what the future might bring. All summer, I had been in charge of everything. Taking care of myself, attending classes, coming and going as I pleased…

Turns out, there was very little I had control of now.

Pride is a funny thing. It's there when you need it, protecting you, keeping you at arms' length from the world at large. And then, when you least expect it, it drops away and leaves you vulnerable and sobbing your eyes out.

"Lina, what's wrong?"

The flood gates opened as I stood there and tried to figure out where to begin. After a few long minutes, I composed myself enough to say, "Josh…woke up…"

"That's great, honey," Dad murmured into my hair.

"I know. It's what I've been waiting all this time for, but…he's different." I clutched a handful of flannel in my hands, grateful for Dad's stability. "He's so different now. I didn't know he was going to be so *different*. I don't think he'll ever be the same." Nothing had ever broken my heart like this before.

Dad's hold on me tightened and I cried into his shirt. The flannel smelled like laundry detergent and for some reason the clean, fresh scent made me cry even harder.

"Oh, baby. You just have to give him time."

"But," I blubbered, "I've already given so much."

"I know, baby. The two of you have been through a lot."

Dad didn't have any magical pearls of wisdom to give me, so we stood at the entrance of the garage and let the uncertainties of life swirl around us.

~~Day 88~~
Day 1

Now that I was in the mood to celebrate life again, I decided to start the days over at the beginning. Because that's what today was. A new beginning.

Sorry I haven't written anything all day. There has been so much going on that I haven't had a minute to myself to crack open the ole journal.

Well, Josh, you did it. You finally did it. After nearly three months of flawlessly imitating Sleeping Beauty, you finally woke up. This has to be the happiest day of my life. I've been writing in this journal for what seems like forever, but I can't even put into words how relieved and excited I am.

All I can say is thank you, thank you, thank you...

Today was also an ending. The journal had been a good place to put my thoughts when Josh wasn't there to talk to, but now that he was awake, there was no need to document everything.

It would feel strange to stop keeping a journal of every day's activities, but I guess in the end I had been doing it more for me than for him.

Chapter Fifteen

Even though Josh had remembered my name that first day, the next few times he woke up, his cognitive function was impaired. Or at least that's what Dr. Patel called it.

Impaired cognitive function.

To know that the word 'impaired' was now being associated with Josh was a hard pill to swallow.

Little shards of anger whittled their way past my defenses and I cursed how a senseless accident could leave a strong, young man little more than a confused child. Now he couldn't even get a drink of water without someone helping him.

Dr. Patel explained a bunch of other stuff to me, too. He said that Josh would most likely emerge with physical and mental difficulties. His muscles would be weak and he had a severe loss of muscle tone. Muscular atrophy was the scientific term. Josh had a long road of recovery ahead of him and would require special medical attention.

Those were the facts. I didn't want to believe them, to believe that Josh might somehow be left permanently damaged, but they were the facts.

Reality set in. Josh wasn't the same boy he used to be. And he might not ever be. That was okay. I wasn't the same girl from before the accident either.

The next day, and the next day after that, Josh opened his eyes again. And I was right there to offer him all the encouragement and motivation he could ever need.

Eventually, he started to turn his head when he saw me and when he heard my voice. Then he was able to nod his head. After that, he started tracking me as I moved around the room.

Every day was a new day and every day Josh made more progress. Mostly it was things that no one else would notice, but to me they were monumental. Like regaining his smile, his eyes twinkling the way they used to like he was privy to some inside joke. I noticed.

Dr. Patel also warned me that Josh might not recover from the coma and that if he did he might remain in a vegetative state. The phrase made me think of carrots and celery, and the limp veggies Aunt Rhoda had put in the overcooked beef stew she'd served me one day at my house. Josh was no vegetable. From the way his body was lashing out in his sleep, he was still fighting with every breath to stay alive.

Things might get worse before they start to get better. Agatha's voice echoed inside my brain.

Last week, Josh had been too weak to hold his hand up and now he was trying to pull out his IV. And then the kicking started. He kicked his feet like he was drowning and trying to kick himself up to the surface.

I talked to him in the most soothing voice I could manage. "Sshh," I cooed, even though he hadn't said anything. "It's okay." Physical touch seemed to have a calming effect and I swiped my thumb over his knuckles. Back and forth. Back and forth.

It's going to be okay.

Agatha handed me a damp washcloth and I gently patted it over the sweat on his forehead. Warren was back at work and Catherine was "sleeping in." The united front they'd formed the other day had crumbled as soon as they realized their son was damaged goods.

Josh was living life in the slow lane now when we all knew he was meant to drive faster than the posted speed limit.

If I thought Josh's emergence from the coma would magically dissolve Catherine's drinking problem, I'd have been wrong. If anything, she fell apart even more. Maybe with Josh awake, she had come face-to-face with her shortcomings as a mother.

"Josh, listen to me. Listen to the sound of my voice and try to calm yourself down. Please stop pulling at your IVs. They're going to have to restrain you if you don't stop. They'll have to sedate you, Josh."

Hadn't he spent enough time sedated?

As if he could hear me, he stopped kicking and began to rock from side to side.

"You're going to be all right, okay?"

"Where...?" It looked like he was staring off into space, but at least he was speaking.

"You're at home," I said. "Safe in your bedroom."

"...don't...remember."

"Well, you're in luck, my friend. Because I remember everything."

He blinked and looked at me again. His eyes didn't smile, or light up, or do any of the things they used to do. But that was okay. We had all the time in the world to get back to that point.

"You are Joshua Warren Thornton. You are seventeen years old and you are going into your senior year at August Lake High School. You love sports. Hockey especially. And your favorite player is Cody Lambert, the Razors captain. You have a smile that can light up a room..."

That evening, I sat and talked to Josh long after his eyes closed and he drifted off to sleep again. He stopped kicking and he stopped pulling at the tubes attached to his body. I talked and I sang and I never stopped holding his hand.

Hours later, he woke up again a little less disoriented.

"Car?" His voice was a hoarse whisper.

"I'm right here, Josh. I never left."

"If..." He still paused a lot in the middle of sentences like he was trying to fit the pieces together. "If...I don't...make it—"

"Josh!" Anger and fear wound its way around my heart. He couldn't talk like that! He'd made it too far to give up now. "You are. You. Are. Going. To. Make. It. You were in a terrible accident. You had bones broken and your body was bruised and scraped up. You were asleep for a long time so that your body could heal from everything it went through. But you woke up.

"That was half the battle, Josh. Waking up. And you did it because you are strong and you are brave. You aren't going to *die* now, not after everything. Not after how hard you fought to come back. I won't let you give up. I won't let you."

He blinked once and when he opened his eyes, he searched my face.

"Don't even think about dying," I rasped. "It's not an option."

He blinked again and looked down at his hands like he was ashamed to say the words out loud.

"I'm not going anywhere," I informed him in a stern tone. "So, when you have thoughts of giving up, just stop it. Stop it, Josh. You've come too far to give up now."

"But…it hurts." His voice scratched like 40-grit sandpaper.

I swallowed hard. "I understand that. But you've never let pain stand in your way *before*. And you aren't going to *now*. Remember when you broke your wrist in eighth grade?"

Slowly, Josh shook his head. As long as his memory remained fuzzy and disjointed, it was up to me to remind him of the past.

"Dakota slammed you into the boards when you were playing hockey and a bone in your wrist snapped. You told me that you could actually *hear* it break. I don't know if that was really true or if you were just trying to gross me out. Anyway, you had to wear a cast for weeks, but it didn't stop you from playing. You were out there on the ice the next day skating drills during your free time, even though Coach Wrigley benched you.

"You're being too hard on yourself. All of this is going to take time." They were the same words Agatha had said to me right after they brought Josh home from the hospital.

These things take time, Carli.

"Yeah, it's going to hurt, Josh. And you're going to have to learn a ton of stuff over again, but giving up isn't an option. Just *try*. You've got it in you to succeed and I'll be right here with you every step of the way. I'm here for you, Josh." Always and forever, remember?

He blinked a few more times and I wondered if my words were falling on deaf ears.

"*Please*," I begged him when he still didn't speak.

"I'll try." He mumbled the words so softly that I barely heard them.

Whether he shouted them from the rooftops or simply mouthed them to me silently, they still gave me hope.

The journal I was supposed to abandon was open in front of me, a blank page staring me in the face. I couldn't give up on writing in it. Not when I needed it the most.

Josh,

The words were hard to write and I had to force my pen to move across the paper.

You are the best part of me. If anything happens to you...

I know I shouldn't entertain negative thoughts like that, but if anything happens to you I don't know what I'd do. And I really don't want to find out. Please don't put me through that kind of anguish.

You have to keep fighting, Josh. Just keep hanging on.

Even if you can't find it in your heart to love me back, please do this one thing for me.

I love you.

Carlina

I didn't know what I expected things to be like after Josh woke up. It wasn't like I'd have him to myself forever. Eventually his mom even had to limit his visitors because he was too weak to see them all in one day. Everyone wanted to see him now that he was cognizant. All the people who had shunned him for the past few months practically beat a path to his bed, eager to give him gifts and flowers. It seemed strange to see his room full of colorful bouquets of roses and daisies. I don't think anyone would have given a seventeen-year-old boy flowers for any other occasion.

Friends—all of them except Kendall and Hunter—gathered around his bed, smiling and cracking jokes to lighten the mood. I didn't blame them for avoiding him for months. I was just glad they were here now, showing their support and making his face light up.

Even though he'd put on a happy face for his friends, his eyes were droopy and I knew he was exhausted. He didn't want them to see how weak he was.

Agatha—dear, dear Agatha—must have sensed his struggle because she quickly shooed them out of the room, telling them that Josh needed his rest and thanked them for dropping by. My heart bottomed out as I watched his body sag against the pillows, relieved.

Day after day, Josh made progress and began physical therapy. Like a newborn baby, he had to relearn how to do everything. He had to learn to walk again. A lot of things were familiar, but everything was new. Therapy was his new reality. Physical therapy, speech therapy, occupational therapy, pool therapy. Some PT was done at home and he went to a rehab facility for the rest. Although it was grueling, he never complained once. Between all the therapy session there wasn't much time for anything else.

Despite his physical limitations, he never stopped fighting. In fact, he was so determined to regain his mobility that he pushed himself to the point of exhaustion.

When he had the time and the energy, we played video games together. Battling it out on a faux race track helped restore his hand-eye coordination.

He still slept *a lot* and tired quickly during the short bursts when he was awake. His circulation wasn't back to one-hundred percent and he was cold all the time.

His long list of ailments included headaches, dizziness and concentration problems. His motor skills were off and his emotions were out of whack from being comatose for so long. Sometimes he confused memories with dreams.

"Sometimes the words that are in my brain aren't the ones that come out of my mouth," he complained to Dr. Patel.

And yet Dr. Patel seemed impressed with Josh's progress. "With your level of motivation you will probably get there a bit faster than average."

But it wasn't fast enough for Josh.

There was no way he'd be well enough for school when it started in early September and I think that was what frustrated him most of all. He'd have to make up all the final exams he'd missed in May—the ones required for him to move on to twelfth grade—and he'd have to continue to work with a tutor.

Not all of Josh's body woke up. His left hand was partially paralyzed and was always numb, tingling like it was asleep.

"My whole left side is messed up, Car. My leg still doesn't work right and my arm is numb all the time."

"It's all part of you now."

"A crappy souvenir, if you ask me."

After everything he'd been through, his lingering injuries seemed like a small price to pay.

"Thanks for taking care of my dog for me," Josh said as he patted Gordie's belly. "I know my mom wasn't the one feeding him this whole time."

"He never left your side. Except for when you had a fever, he actually came to my house to get me."

"Did you think I was going to die?"

Every day.

"I knew you were too stubborn to give up," I managed to say.

"I lost out on so much time," he said, sounding discouraged. "The therapy sucks and I'm getting sick of it. Why did this have to happen?"

The whys of the situation were irrelevant. What mattered was how he was going to keep finding the strength to get better.

"Maybe you were in a coma for so long that you forgot who you are. Maybe you don't remember how amazing and funny and *stubborn* you were, but I'm here to remind you. I loved the boy who was strong enough to find a way out of the darkness and wake up, flaws and all. And I love you still."

There was nothing like laying your heart out on a silver platter to get your pulse racing.

This is me telling you that I love you, Josh.

"It's okay that you're a little bit broken. It's okay that everything is more difficult than you remember. Because you never wished for things to be easier when you were doing them *before*. You liked things to be difficult. You *enjoyed* the challenge. Because what good is anything if you don't have to work hard for it. Not just anyone can develop the skills to play hockey or do backflips off the dock.

"Only people with *courage* can do the cool stuff," I quoted his words back to him.

There was a flicker of recognition in his eyes and I knew he remembered.

"I remember," he said.

And that was all I needed to hear.

The baby steps Josh made in therapy were huge leaps for someone who had been in a coma for so long. Frustrated and mentally and physically drained, he lay back in his bed every evening, his body shaking from exhaustion.

"You're doing great," I told him.

He gave me an exasperated look. "My progress…isn't fast enough." He still stumbled over his words occasionally, but every day he sounded more and more like his old self.

"For now it is."

"What do you know about it?" he said, rolling his eyes.

He was right. How could I know anything about progress when all I had done was sit by his bed, thinking about how I had survived the accident with barely a scratch, while Josh was left to fight for whatever meager pieces were left of his life?

"Believe me," I told him sternly, "I know enough." Just because he was fragile didn't mean I was going to sit back and let him walk all over me. He had enough people babying him these days.

"I have the strength of a newborn, the stamina of an eighty-year-old, and the endurance of a turtle." He went to sleep in the best shape of his life and woke up a vegetable with a side of noodle limbs.

"You were in bed for three months. What do you expect?"

"I could always count on you to tell it like it is."

I wished I could tell him how things were between us. How I wanted them to be. But even *I* didn't know the answer to *that* riddle.

"You'll get back to where you were." Eventually.

We'd be able to face anything as long as he was awake to face it with me.

"But what if I don't?" He was agitated. "What if I miss out on the draft? What if I can't ever run again, much less lace up a pair of hockey skates?"

I took a minute to think about my response. Even though he'd been doing nothing but proving how strong he was, he was still fragile in so many areas.

How did you tell your best friend that he probably wouldn't be able to pursue his dreams of playing pro hockey? How was I supposed to tell him that everything he'd ever dreamed of was circling down the drain? But then again, who was I to write him off so quickly? He'd woken up when no one else thought he would, right? So, who was I to say what he could and couldn't accomplish in the future?

An image of Josh flashed through my mind. He was staring up at me from his place on the hockey rink. On the ice was where he was the happiest, I think. Gliding across the blue line, his skates etching tracks into the slick ice. He felt free when he was playing hockey. Like he could conquer anything.

He still could. I would just have to remind him.

"I asked a lot of what-ifs when you were in the coma, too. We just have to take each day at a time. That's what I did to get through."

"One day at a time."

"Yep. And today you promised me a Go Fish rematch."

Josh rolled his eyes.

"See," I said cheerfully. "You're making tons of progress. You're already rolling your eyes at me and everything."

"Just deal the stupid cards already, Carlina."

Chapter Sixteen

Time. As it ticks by in seconds, it's hardly noticed at all. When those seconds are clumped together in minutes, hours, and days, that's when you start to realize how quickly time really passes us by.

Nature demonstrates the passage of time by the changing of the seasons. Leaves change color, temperatures fluctuate, then plummet, and the days become shorter. The sun doesn't blaze as hotly in the sky and you don't have to wait for it to slide behind the mountains at the end of the day to get relief from the pulsing heat.

September arrived right on schedule. The sky acted like it might rain and kept its vibrant blue covered up with dark grey clouds. My tank tops and shorts were soon replaced with long sleeves and jeans. Snuggling beneath a fuzzy blanket became my favorite pastime again and it was a welcome change to replace ice cold drinks with steaming hot cocoa. Not only had I aced my summer school finals, but I had also passed my driving test with flying colors.

The day after Labor Day, I started school with the rest of the students from ALHS and subsequently became the go-to for info about Josh Thornton's miraculous recovery. Popularity was foreign to me and random kids asking me about Josh took some getting used to.

Going to school without Josh was an odd feeling, but we wouldn't have had any classes together anyway. I was taking all Advanced Placement classes, kicking my trek to college into high gear. Josh was being homeschooled and a tutor came to his house four days a week.

With my dad spending so much more time at home, and classes and homework eating up most of my time, I didn't spend every waking moment at Josh's house like I used to.

The months following Josh's awakening weren't easy, but there was no time to stop and indulge in any "why me" episodes. School was back in full swing and the clock kept on ticking, moving us forward, whether we wanted to go that way or not.

I tried to step back and let Josh do things on his own timeline, and by October he'd far and away surpassed Dr. Patel's expectations. It should have come as a surprise that he was sitting up on his own and able to use a wheelchair six weeks after he'd woken up, but knowing Josh, he wasn't about to lay around and let everyone wait on him hand and foot for the rest of his life.

Three weeks after progressing to a wheelchair, Josh was up and walking with the help of a walker.

Perhaps he drew the extra strength he needed from me. I might have perceived Josh's stubbornness as a negative trait before, but it was part of what drove him—along with sheer determination—to make the kind of progress he achieved.

Josh's nurses hung on as long as they could, but eventually Josh got to the point where he didn't need 24-hour care. Mamie said her goodbyes in a flurry of a language we didn't understand, tears, and more baklava than we could possibly eat in a year.

When it was Agatha's turn to say goodbye, my throat tightened to the point where I couldn't speak. She'd been my rock during this whole ordeal and now she was moving on to other jobs and other patients.

"Bring it on in here, child." She extended her arms and grinned.

We hugged for a long time and eventually drew away from each other, knowing it was time to say goodbye. She held me at arm's length and I laughed through the tears when I saw the twinkle in her eyes.

"I'll keep in touch," she assured me. "I'm starting a new job tomorrow, caring for a quadriplegic."

"You'll do fine," I said, laughing at how grown up I sounded. I would miss seeing her every day, but she had her own adventure to begin.

"You're an inspiration, Carli."

I swallowed down the lump in my throat. "Me?"

"Yes, you. I told my daughter about you and you inspired her to go back to school and get her teaching certificate. She said that if you could go to summer school, then she could handle night school. It'll be a slow go with her still working full time, but I know she'll do great."

"Thank you, Agatha," I murmured.

With her knitting tucked away in her over-sized tote bag, Agatha waved goodbye one last time and headed out to her truck.

When Josh and I were alone again, he nudged my arm with his elbow. "You two were close," he muttered.

"Yes. Agatha was the only one who didn't think I was crazy for staying by your side."

Looking thoughtful, Josh frowned. Then his lips twitched like he was trying not to smile. "I should have given her a bigger hug."

On my way home from school the next afternoon, I stopped by Josh's house. My dad was having new brakes installed on the Jeep, so I was bike-bound. When I passed Catherine on the deck, she told me to go on up to Josh's room and I didn't think anything of it.

After knocking, I opened the door when I heard Josh's mumbled "Come in."

He wasn't alone.

I jumped back, startled to see that he already had company—of the female variety. And Catherine had instructed me to go in anyway. Thanks a lot, Mama Thornton.

Instead of being huddled together the way a girlfriend and boyfriend should be, Kendall stood on the other side of the room, her arms folded and her chin thrust out defensively. Josh sat in the chair next to his bed, looking like he'd seen better days.

"Oh…sorry," I stuttered. "I'll come back later." I backed out, closed the door behind me and walked outside.

Oh, to be a fly on the wall during that conversation!

Then I remembered their relationship. Boyfriend and girlfriend.

Joshua and Kendall sitting in a tree…

Their lips were probably making up for lost time and there was no way I wanted to see *that*.

How could I be so stupid? If Josh were to choose between us, how was I to know he wouldn't choose Kendall over me?

How could Kendall just waltz in and take her place as his girlfriend when she never once visited him in the hospital, let alone here at his home? I know she was busy being the most popular girl in school, but she could've taken two minutes out of her daily trip to Red Valley Mall to see if her boyfriend was okay. He'd been awake for almost *two* months and she hadn't had the decency to break up with him already. Which was more important? Popularity or people?

I trusted Josh to see the situation as it really was.

While Kendall and Josh were reacquainting their lips— probably, maybe—I rode down to Midway to buy Twinkies because they were Josh's favorite. He had to work his way up to solid food so as not to upset his stomach and he was so hungry all the time that he'd been begging his mom to let him eat tacos from Tico's Tacos. A spongey dessert with absolutely no nutritional value seemed like a good way to tide him over until Catherine caved on the Mexican food.

While I perused the sweet treats, Kendall came around the corner.

"Oh, hello *Carli*." She always said my name like it put a bad taste in her mouth. Which was fine because simply seeing her put a bad taste in mine.

"Hi," I said, gripping the Twinkie I was holding.

"I'm surprised you're still not at Josh's. You practically spent your whole *summer* at his house."

I squeezed my fingers around the Twinkie. What did it matter to her *where* I spent my summer? She seemed to care more about my whereabouts than she did Josh's.

I wanted to keep my mouth shut, I really did. Avoiding confrontation was something I was good at, something I excelled in. But looking at her scrunched up face and the way her punctuated voice cut through my head, I couldn't let her comments go.

"It's called friendship," I bit out. "You might want to try it sometime."

Kendall shoved a fist onto her hip and glared at me. "What do you know about *anything*, Carli Thornley? Just because you practically have the same last name as Josh doesn't mean he likes you more than a friend."

"You're supposed to be his *girlfriend* and yet you never went to visit him *once*, not even when he was in the hospital. I don't know about *you*, but I care about *my* friends and don't just *abandon* them when the going gets tough."

Her eyes widened and her lips curled into a disgusted scowl. She opened her mouth to put up a fight, but no words came out. I had left her shocked and speechless.

Left with nothing else to say, I stormed out of the store, the bell clattering wildly on the door. I ran around to the back of the building and leaned against the wall. A few seconds later, only when I heard Kendall's car start and pull out onto the highway, did I finally allowed myself to take a breath. I was shaking and tears burned the backs of my eyes.

I looked down at the squished Twinkie in my palm and sighed. I'd destroyed Josh's favorite snack cake and to make matters worse, I'd forgotten to pay for it.

After making sure the coast was clear, I went back inside the store. Abram, the owner, shot me a grin, which surprised me a little after what had happened.

"Sorry I made a scene," I apologized, hanging my head.

Abram was still grinning. "You didn't. We were the only ones in the store. She deserved it anyway."

So, I wasn't the only one who knew what the real Kendall Lamont was like.

I went to the Hostess display and picked out another Twinkie. "I forgot to pay for this," I said, holding up the smashed package.

"Don't worry 'bout it. It's on the house."

Ignoring the offer, I slapped enough cash for both Twinkies on the counter and walked back outside.

Sure, I'd made my point clear, but frivolous girls like Kendall Lamont didn't give two rips about what I thought.

My high and mighty speech to Kendall didn't make me feel much better about the situation, but at least I hadn't let her steamroll right over me. Dad would be proud.

Later, when I walked into Josh's bedroom, I was still a little shaky. I'd never told anyone off before. Yeah, I'd thought about it plenty of times, but the words never actually left my mouth. All in all, I guess it was worth it to see the astonished look on Kendall's upturned face.

"I brought snacks," I announced happily, wondering if the guilt was apparent in my expression.

"What happened to *that* one?" Josh asked, looking at the crushed Twinkie in my right hand. "You ride over it with your bike?"

I could have lied and said yes—it would have been a lot easier—but I decided to tell him the truth. I might've been a lousy best friend, but at least I was honest. Honest to a fault.

"I had a little run-in with Kendall," I answered, handing him the good Twinkie. "And the Twinkie just happened to be a casualty."

The wrapper crinkled as he turned the Twinkie over in his hands. "What, did you throw it at her?"

"*No*," I answered defensively.

Although, on second thought, that might've been more satisfying. Except I definitely would have opened it first so that the white cream could stick in her hair. *That* would have ruined her day for sure.

Feeling embarrassed and slightly ashamed, I told Josh what had happened at Midway Market. Instead of telling me to get out and never come back, Josh grinned from ear to ear.

"Why are you so happy?" I asked. "Shouldn't you be defending her honor or something? She's your *girlfriend*."

"Not anymore. I broke up with her." He said it in a calm, matter-of-fact way like it was no big deal. "I heard she spent the summer with a bunch of other guys."

I buried my face in my hands and mumbled, "I can't believe this." Then I lifted my face and looked at him head-on. "So, I finally got up the nerve to tell her off and you'd already broken up with her?" I shrieked.

Josh opened the package and shoved a Twinkie at me. "Here, to the victor belong the spoils."

"Shouldn't you be broken up over this? Why aren't you inconsolable?"

He shrugged. "Being in a coma gives you a new perspective on life."

"*Perspective*?" He just broke up with his pretty, popular girlfriend and he was telling me about perspective?

"Yeah," he said. He took a bite, chewed, closed his eyes and savored the flavor, and finally swallowed. "She was too high-maintenance anyway. And she'd never eat food like this with me. She'd spend the whole time whining and lecturing me about the calories."

"Well," I said, satisfied by his explanation, "I deserve this." I waved my demolished Twinkie at him and patted my thigh. "Calories shmalories. My little outburst had to have burned off several hundred calories, so I should be okay."

"Glad we got that cleared up," he smirked.

After a few seconds I asked, "So, why were you with her in the first place?" It took a lot of effort on my part to sound curious and not repulsed.

"I was being stupid," he answered with a shrug. "My brother bet me I couldn't get the head cheerleader to go out with me."

"Blake put you up to it?" So much for not sounding repulsed.

"It was just a friendly wager between brothers."

The Twinkie did a long somersault inside my esophagus. "You're disgusting."

"And you're sweet for bringing me Twinkies."

Chapter Seventeen

Friday after school, I stopped by Josh's house, opened his door, and walked in without thinking twice about knocking. The only thing Josh was wearing was a pair of boxers. He wasn't wearing a shirt.

I'd just walked in on a half-naked Josh.

"Jeez, Carli," he sputtered. "Don't you knock?"

Some habits were hard to break. After what I found on the other side of this door the last time I knocked, I should have known better.

"Sorry." I backed out of the room, shut the door and leaned against the wall as my brain processed what I'd just seen. Josh's body. I'd seen him with no shirt on before. At the lake and the pool. But now instead of muscles, his bones were harsh angles against his skin. His ribs poked through his skin. He didn't have an athlete's body anymore. He had the body of a living corpse.

Already huffing from exertion, he yanked open the door and I held my breath. Things were awkward between us now where they weren't before. Somehow I had thought things would just go back to normal after he woke up. Now we were like strangers sometimes, dancing around the fact that we used to be best friends. Either we were growing apart or simply taking a while to snap all the pieces back together.

He had put on a shirt and his face was wearing a scowl. "You didn't have to leave." He swayed because his balance was still off and he rested his weight on the walker for support.

"I'm sorry I didn't knock. I've been so used to coming and going when I pleased that I didn't even think about it."

"It's okay."

He waved me inside and I followed him into his room.

Determined to stand on his own as often as he could, he stepped away from the walker. "Did you see my scars?"

"No." I knew they'd taken a lot of glass out of his back, but I hadn't seen the proof.

Josh pulled off his shirt again and turned around. Several gashes on the back of his shoulder and below his shoulder blades marred his skin. A bigger gash ran from his neck to the small of his back. It must have been from when the car door frame caved in on him.

"Go ahead," he urged. "Touch them."

My body went rigid at the command and every emotion I'd ever experienced swirled through my head at once. "No, that's okay."

I don't want to hurt you.

"Touch them. It doesn't hurt at all."

Slowly, only because he'd asked me to, I reached out and ran my fingers over the jagged, puckered skin. The skin around the scars was pale and smooth. His skin was warm, but the feel of his wounds left me feeling cold.

I dropped my hand, instantly sad that the accident had left permanent scars on his beautiful skin. He had been cursed to wear a reminder of that horrible day on his body for keeps.

"Weird, huh?" he asked.

"Yeah."

Out of breath from even the smallest movement, he struggled and finally got his shirt back on. "How 'bout you? You get any scars?"

My dad liked to tell people that I survived the accident without a scratch. But the truth was, I did have a scratch. A scar on my forearm from broken glass. I itched at the scar now, wondering why I'd been spared.

I held my arm out. "Just this." The little line on my arm was like comparing raspberries to watermelons.

Josh's fingers traced over the small scar and I almost forgot to breathe. "Gnarly," he said with a smirk.

Automatically, without thinking, my hand shot out to smack him, but I quickly pulled it back before making contact.

"I'm not so fragile anymore, Car."

"I know." I just didn't want to be the cause of any setbacks.

"What about you, Car? Everybody fusses over me and I think they forget it happened to you, too."

My heart filled with admiration. Josh was right. Just because I wasn't physically hurt, everyone sort of forgot I'd been in the accident, too.

"I'm fine sitting back and letting you be the attention hog. I don't want anyone fussing over me anyway."

"Tell me about the accident." He wheeled his desk chair around to face me and sat down. "My mom won't tell me anything. She keeps saying all that matters is that I'm okay. Do you remember it?"

I could account for every second of that day.

"Yes," I said, my voice barely above a whisper.

His brows furrowed and he leaned forward, resting his arms on the tops of his thighs. "What happened, Car?"

I sat down on the edge of the window seat and clasped my hands together. When that didn't feel right, I stood up again and walked over to inspect his trophies. A part of me—the part I tried to keep locked away—wondered if he'd ever win another one.

"You really want to hear about it?"

No one else did. Anytime I tried to tell anyone the story, they cringed and begged me to stop talking. It was too gruesome, too depressing. Too nerve-wrackingly real. So I kept it bottled inside.

"Yeah. I want you to tell me what happened."

What really happened.

He didn't have to say the words for me to understand. He was asking me not to sugarcoat it.

Tell me the truth.

"Okay." I turned to face him. "Well, that afternoon you picked me up at my house so we could go to the Raptors game together. We were driving on August Hwy where the bridge is. You know that spot where—"

Josh nodded and I continued. "We were arguing about which band was better live in concert. Crush 21 or The Eggs."

"The Eggs," Josh said quickly. "Obviously."

I smiled. "Right. And I said Crush 21."

No matter how much we had joked around that day, Josh hadn't behaved recklessly. If anything, I remember glancing over at the speedometer and making a comment about how he was obeying the posted speed limit for once. He gave me a feigned shocked *pshaw* and dove into a reenactment of *Rainman* about how he was a good driver. In return, I smacked him on the shoulder 1) because he was being a smartass and 2) because it gave me an excuse to touch him.

"I looked over at you to argue and I remember seeing an SUV coming toward us. It was going so fast. Before I could open my mouth to say anything *BAM* it hit us and pushed us right into the bridge embankment. It was so loud and then I opened my eyes and the airbag was in my face. I had a difficult time breathing because the whole car was smashed around us. It was weird because all I can remember is how *loud* it was. And how quiet *you* were.

"The worst part was waiting for them to cut us out. I was so afraid we'd get smashed even more. I don't remember much from during the ride to the hospital. I was pretty out of it. They kept me overnight, but there wasn't anything wrong with me, so I was released the next day. You were in the ICU for a while and they wouldn't let me see you. Finally, your mom took me in to your hospital room. There were so many tubes and wires and machines hooked up to you..."

"What happened to the guy who hit us?"

It would have been easier to write down the answer in the journal than to say the words out loud, but I hadn't told Josh about the journal yet. I guess I wanted to make sure he was focused on the future and not distracted by the things that happened in the past first.

"I guess he had a history of mental illness and they think he was making a run for the bridge and we happened to get in the way. They told him he'd be charged with vehicular manslaughter if you didn't wake up. When he heard what he did, he...he took his own life in the hospital and finished the job."

I felt sick inside like I might throw up. I hadn't wanted the guy to kill himself. It didn't bring closure to anything. Josh was still alive and kicking and that man's senseless death helped nobody.

Josh looked down at his hands. "I'm sorry you had to go through all of that alone."

There had been many times, when I'd stood and stared at the wrecked Camaro parked in Gus's junkyard, that I had thought the same thing.

"I wasn't *completely* alone," I reassured him now. "You were there, you just couldn't hear me." I knelt beside him.

For a split second he looked confused to see me there. And then he touched my face. "You're here. When that SUV crashed into us I thought I lost you forever."

"I'm here," I whispered. "I never left."

He blinked a few times and squinted at me. "I remember now. I tried to reach for you, but then everything went black." He lowered his hand from my face and the connection was lost.

For a brief moment I thought he might tell me what I'd been waiting to hear, but he asked another question instead.

"What happened to my car?"

"It was towed over to Gus's junkyard."

"Have you seen it?"

"Yeah, it's pretty bad. I asked Gus to keep it because I thought you might want to see it someday. Looking at it, it's hard to believe we made it out alive."

Dozens of times I had walked around to the front of the car to the passenger side. The little space inside barely looked big enough for a baby, much less a full grown me. And yet, I had sat there after the accident, scrunched up in the contorted metal and waited. I had looked over and Josh was twisted like a pretzel and slumped over. I talked to him then, too. I figured maybe he'd get so sick of hearing my voice that he'd wake up already. Even though I was usually quiet, ever since that day I kept talking, worried that if I stopped, so would Josh's heartbeat.

"Exactly how long was I out for?"

I took a deep breath and exhaled slowly. "Eighty-eight days."

It took him a few seconds to process the numbers, and then, "Jeez. My mom wouldn't tell me that either."

Why not? I wondered. What exactly was Catherine trying to protect him from? Didn't he deserve to know exactly what had happened to him to make him the way he was today?

"My mom said you came to see me every day. That you were the only one to come see me. It's nice to know you were there for me even if I didn't know it at the time."

I shrugged it off. "We're best friends," I said lamely. He was so much more than that. But how could I put it into simple words?

"We're a lot more than friends, Carli."

The way his voice said the words made my heart jerk inside my chest. All I could do was swallow and hope he kept talking.

"I remember…I remember you talking to me. I didn't always know what you were saying, but I could hear your voice."

"I hoped as much."

"I don't remember hearing anyone's voice but yours."

Probably because no one had spent the time to talk to him as much as I had.

"How was your dad's trip to Reno?"

I froze and my jaw hung open like the hinge had come undone. "How did you know he was in Reno?" Deep down I already knew, but I needed to hear him say it.

"You must have told me."

"Yeah," I sputtered. "While you were *unconscious*."

He shrugged it off like it was nothing.

"You *heard* me?" My voice raised a few octaves and actually cracked. I swallowed and cleared my throat.

Josh smirked at my croaking and I resisted the urge to smack him upside the head.

"I must have."

"What else do you remember?"

Another shrug. "I dunno. I can't remember off the top of my head. I don't remember a lot of things. Especially anything about the accident. Or what we were doing right before it."

"You were talking about how much you were looking forward to the new Eggs album. That reminds me." I hopped out of my seat and plugged his iPod into its speaker dock. "This is the first thing I wanted you to hear when you woke up."

Seconds later, the newest track from Josh's favorite band drifted from the speakers. The Eggs had really stepped it up for the new album and it was almost impossible to keep from belting out the catchy lyrics at the top of your lungs.

Except Josh didn't look ready to party. He looked…confused.

"This sounds familiar. I think I've already heard it."

"But it's brand new. It just came out in July."

"Did you play it for me?"

I swallowed. "I did."

"Then that's when I first heard it."

What else did he remember? Did he remember what I told him about the Falls? Did he remember me holding his hand? Did he remember me telling him *I love you*?

Would he want to remember those things?

"Did you sing to me?" He scrunched up his face and thought about it. "I remember someone singing to me and it sure wasn't my mom."

I felt heat rush to my face as I blushed a furious shade of red, I'm sure.

Josh playfully smacked my shoulder. "You *did*, didn't you? You sang to your dear old friend Josh."

"I might have," I answered softly.

"I knew it!" he said triumphantly. "What did you sing?"

"I'm not telling you," I sputtered.

"C'mon, Car. Tell me what it was. It's, like, one of the only things I remember."

"It was just something my mom used to sing to me when I was little," I fibbed. He wouldn't want to hear the Crush 21 song I'd altered for him.

"Sing it."

"No!" The only reason I'd sung to him was because I thought for sure there was a possibility he couldn't hear me. I sure as heck didn't think he'd actually *remember* it and ask me to perform it live in front of him like some kind of circus freak.

"Do it. Sing me a jaunty tune!" He poked me in the ribs, in that spot he knew was extra ticklish, and proceeded to tickle me.

I squealed and we tumbled down onto the bed, a tangle of flailing arms and legs and I knew he wouldn't let up until I agreed to sing. Our arms wound around each other and suddenly he went still. His face was close to mine. So close, I could count his eyelashes if I wanted to. His breath puffed out in warm puffs on my face. He leaned closer and I closed my eyes as his lips touched mine. The kiss was brief and soft and tender.

After a few heartbeats, he pulled away and I opened my eyes and blinked. I'd only ever been kissed by one other boy in my whole entire life. Connor Davies. He kissed me next to the gym (it was technically just a peck on the cheek) and his family moved to Cleveland a week later. Josh had just kissed me on the lips like it was the most natural thing in the world.

"Sing the song, Carli," he said softly.

I wanted to talk about the kiss or do it again and he was asking me to sing for him. Something I would never understand. So I decided to make sure he wouldn't forget about the kiss. When else would I get another chance like this?

My heart pounded in my chest and a tingly feeling crept through my seventeen-year-old body. I leaned forward and touched my lips to his. He didn't pull away like I thought he might, like I was afraid he would, but he curved his hand around my waist and held me close to him. He kissed me back.

His lips moved against mine and we kissed for what could have been hours, but was probably only seconds. His tongue darted out and I parted my lips.

All of the fear, the "How will I know what to do? Where do I put my hands?" uncertainty flew out the window and it all came naturally.

I was kissing Josh Thornton!

It felt like there was a pinball loose inside my body hitting the bumpers and being whacked around with the flippers. *Ding! Clang!*

When I thought I might lose myself in a monsoon of hormones, I gently pulled back and rested my forehead against his and sighed. His hand rubbed my back, up and down, and we just laid there on his bed until our breathing returned to normal.

"Sing the song, Carli."

How could I refuse? I would do anything for him. And that included singing him a Crush 21 song slightly out of tune and completely embarrassed.

"It wasn't a song my mom used to sing to me. It was actually a Crush 21 song." Maybe that little tidbit would be enough for him to drop the subject altogether.

"Sing it anyway."

No such luck.

The song was titled *When She's Gone*. To make it appropriate for Josh, I had changed the word *she* to *he*.

I think about you all day, but when the sun goes down, it's worse
Then the moon looks down, it's like a curse
When the sun goes down, it hurts
When he's gone and there's no more sunlight,
No more blue skies
Everything is gray
And when he's gone
I can't remember how it feels to smile
There is no need to smile
He's gone.
I can't make him come back
Bring back the colors,
Bring back the sun, the laughter
His smile
He's gone

Even though my voice shook, I sang the song. And Josh kissed me again when I was finished.

Chapter Eighteen

Walking on air was an expression I never fully understood until Josh kissed me. The walk up to his room the next day felt like I was indeed walking on Cloud nine. Anxious to find out if I'd dreamed the whole thing, I had made the ride to his house in record time. Gus might be the best mechanic in town, but he took his sweet time working on the Jeep.

After knocking on Josh's door, I walked in to find him frantically searching through his desk drawers. "Where's my iPod?" he snapped.

"Oh, I have it," I stammered.

He scrunched up his face in confusion. "What for?"

"I wanted to download the new Sick Puppies album for you." To help keep him motivated, I had made sure his iPod was updated with all his favorite music. "They got a new lead singer and—"

"Well, I want it back."

I blinked at his harsh tone and then slid my backpack from my shoulders. "Here, I'll get it out of my backpack."

Clearly agitated, he waved his hand like it was no big deal and climbed into bed. "Don't bother. You know what? Why don't you just get a life, Carli."

What?

His words jammed into my eardrums like a month's worth of wax.

Get a life? Didn't he understand? He *was* my life.

Whether he liked it or not, we shared a bond. We did before the accident and we sure as heck did now.

He was just having a bad day, I told myself. Everyone had them. Josh was certainly entitled to two or three here and there.

I knew he was freaked out and was dealing with all kinds of strange emotions and that he should talk about them with someone. Preferably me. I also knew that he wouldn't talk until he'd worked through most of it in his own head first.

"I'll, uh…I guess I'll see you tomorrow."

He released an irritated sigh. "Don't bother coming over tomorrow either. Don't come back at all."

Oh.

Oh.

So this wasn't just about a bad mood. This was a forever thing.

"I mean it, Carli." He looked at me with mean, dark eyes. "I don't want to see you. Don't wanna see anyone."

Okay then.

As if I needed to hear the words a second time, Josh graciously went on to repeat them as I stood there rooted in disbelief. It was like a knife to the heart.

"Get a friggin' life, Carli. Don't you have anything better to do than come around *bothering* me every freakin' day?"

In all the years we'd known each other, Josh had never once accused me of bothering him in any way, shape, or form. Now he'd said the word like it was poison in his mouth and he was spitting it out to save himself.

I swallowed and looked into the eyes I'd longed to see for twelve weeks. They were open now and looking back at me like they didn't like what they saw.

"Are you sure this is what you want?" I asked timidly. "Or are you just—"

"I want you to get out."

"Okay." My jaw started to quiver. "I…I'm sorry."

Dismissing me, he flicked his eyes down to the phone in his hand and tapped on the screen.

Feeling like the biggest fool on the planet, I slung my backpack over my shoulder again and prepared to leave. Taking one last look around the room, I committed everything to memory. The bed where we'd shared our first kiss, the fish tank, Gordie panting on the window seat…

On my way out, I looked down at the journal I held in my hand. The book had been an extension of me for so long. And now it was time to let it go. I had brought it over to give to Josh anyway.

With nothing else left to lose, I dropped the journal on Josh's bed along with his iPod and bolted out the door.

On the ride home, my legs felt wooden, but I pedaled as fast as I could, away from the one person who used to "get" me. The one person who made me feel giddy and full of nervous butterflies.

After the accident, every day sort of blended in with the next like a painting that had been left out in the rain. Now, I could feel the blood pumping rapidly through my veins and the air whooshing in and out of my lungs. I was awake and alive, but Josh wanted me to get a life. A life where I wouldn't bother him and upset him with my presence.

Deep down, I knew he was probably just upset about something, but his words had cut me to the quick. He'd meant them, I know he meant them. He didn't want me around anymore—or at least for now—and there was absolutely nothing I could do about it.

I wanted to be mad at him, but I probably would've been more than a little perturbed as well if I was the one recovering after a coma.

As I made the turn onto my street, I regretted leaving the journal with him. I had just given him access to my personal thoughts and feelings, all laid out, naked and vulnerable. Was I some kind of masochist or something?

Then I remembered the note I'd left him on the first page. The note I'd been so sure he'd wake up to finally read. Well, now he had a chance to read it all right. There was a possibility he'd think it was stupid, but I hoped he'd appreciate it.

Maybe it would snap him out of whatever mood he was in. Maybe it would make him realize how I really felt about him. Maybe it would make him take back the awful things he'd said.

Dear Josh,

Every day I've sat by your side and willed you to finally wake up and open your eyes. There's so much I want to tell you and so much you're probably wondering about. I've tried to keep track of the important things for you so you don't feel so out of the loop when you wake up.

Some days were easier than others and flew by in the blink of an eye. Others seemed to drag on like there would never be a tomorrow. No matter how discouraged or impatient I got, I tried to be strong for you, just like I know you'd be for me if the situation were reversed.

I'm so glad you're back. I never doubted you once, I swear.

Love,
Carli

Day one...

I ditched my bike on the driveway, ran into the house, and threw myself face first onto my bed.

Day one without Josh.

Day one without my best friend.

Day one of me getting a life.

And doing a lousy job of it.

It was the first full day I'd gone without seeing Josh since before the accident. I sat in my room and tried to study and ended up reading the same sentence over and over until all the words blurred together. Tears sucked when they streamed out of your eyes without your permission. These tears were extra annoying because they were on a mission to make up for lost time.

I had to remind myself that we hadn't shared those special moments in his room *together*. It had been me making those moments alone. It had been me imagining a fictional life together.

For so long I had looked forward to him waking up, but never imagined it would be like this when it finally happened. Josh was telling me to move on. But had I really sat by his side for three months for *this*?

Yesterday, I moped around the house all afternoon and went to bed early. This morning, in the cold light of day, my situation remained bleak. Hopeless. Forlorn. Deplorable.

By evening, things got worse.

I drew in a shuddering breath and wandered around my room, staring at my stuff. Everywhere I looked, Josh was there. My room was full of photos of us together and I didn't have the heart to take them down yet. I had framed my favorite photos and set them on every available surface. On my dresser, there we were with our arms slung over each other's shoulders, grinning into the camera. We'd just come from a hockey game. The Razors' win had felt like our win. On my desk, there was a collage of us taped to the mirror. All those happy smiles and bunny ears reminded me of all the good times we'd shared.

Every time I closed my eyes, I saw the look on Josh's face as he told me to get a life. The image was burned onto the backs of my eyelids and I couldn't find relief from it.

I'd seen him look frustrated before, like when he was trying with all his might to score a goal but the other team kept getting the better of him. Or more recently when he was putting in hours of therapy just to hold his head up on his own. But I'd never seen him so *angry*. Angry at *me*.

After everything we—*I'd*—been through this summer, I guess I felt entitled to *more*. Life sure had a way of leading you on and then pivoting around in the opposite direction so quickly that it gave you whiplash.

Even after everything, I didn't regret sitting by his bedside every chance I hand. I couldn't find it in myself to be cruel enough to wish back all the time I spent watching him sleep. He might not have known that I was there, but *I* knew. I knew what a good friend I was. I knew not to ever lash out at someone who loved me. I knew not to fall in love with someone who didn't love me back.

Or at least I should know by now.

My whole body hurt. Not just my heart and my gut, but my neck and arms ached as if he had physically slapped me. Of course he didn't lay a hand on me, but that look on his face did as much physical damage as mental.

I wished he'd tossed me over a cliff and disposed of me altogether instead. Because now I had to sit here and feel like my insides were decomposing. I'd rather suffer broken bones and crushed organs than to have my heart stomped on with a million pairs of cleats.

I wished he'd never kissed me. Never given me that memory to keep reliving in my head. I'd rather not know how something as simple as a kiss could be so tender and wonderful between us. Except it wasn't simple. It was far from it. Everything was complicated and twisted up and confusing and I didn't think I could survive the aching in my chest.

Now I couldn't help but associate good things with their bad counterparts. Every time I thought about the kiss we shared, all I saw was that cold look in his eyes when he told me to get a life.

Chapter Nineteen

The next the morning I had a visitor, but it wasn't who I was expecting.

Who had I been expecting? Josh to come rolling up to my door in his wheelchair or shuffling up the driveway with his walker? Was I really expecting him to visit me and apologize to me after telling me he never wanted to see me again?

Delusional and depressed. That was me in a nutshell.

Gordie sat at the back door, guarding my bike like it was the Hope Diamond. He looked so cute waiting there, his freakishly long tongue lolling out of his mouth. Gordie always looked like he had a severe case of bedhead and today was no exception.

I had to force myself not to smile at his blatant attempt to bring Josh and me back together.

"Go home, Gordie," I said sternly.

Even though I knew he knew what I was telling him to do, he continued to sit there and look at me with that goofy grin on his face. Wonder who he'd learned it from.

"Go home, Gordie," I repeated. "Your little ploy to get me to go to Josh's house isn't going to work."

I'd already seen the last of the Thornton Estate on August Lake. Of that, I was sure of.

The second his master's name left my mouth, Gordie tilted his head to the side, obviously recognizing the word.

"Things are complicated right now and I don't have time for your shenanigans," I scolded.

The truth of the matter was that I had all the time in the world. Today was Saturday and I didn't have a thing to do besides homework. And I was planning on putting it off until Sunday night like any good teenage procrastinator.

"You know, you're gonna get yourself run over if you keep running around town like this."

Gordie listened intently to my words, waiting patiently for the ones he wanted to hear.

It didn't take long for his patience to pay off.

"All right," I said reluctantly. "Let's go."

Gordie jumped up and twisted around in a few 360s while I wheeled my bike out onto the driveway.

Not enough time had passed yet for me to feel comfortable coming face-to-face with Josh, but if that's what it took to make sure Gordie arrived home safely, then so be it. I couldn't just let the dog play in traffic because he was too pigheaded to go back home.

"I'll ride with you as far at the Lake Forest Road street sign and then you're on your own."

Content with my actions, the stubborn mutt trotted beside me and I took off in the direction of Josh's house.

"Just so you know, I'm not going in with you. I'm just dropping you off and going about my own business. I have my own life, you know." And I was determined to prove it to myself and to Josh.

Gordie didn't answer. Instead, he kept his head down and concentrated on his panting.

"You've really gotta stop coming over to my house, Gord. Now that…"

Josh and I aren't speaking.

I swallowed down the lump in my throat. How had Josh and I reached this place in our relationship? How had we gotten here? How had I let this happen?

"…things are *different*," I continued, "we aren't going to be doing the things we used to."

We aren't going to visit each other or text each other or talk to each other anymore. We're going to go our own separate ways and…

And what?

A gust of wind whooshed around me, causing tendrils of hair to escape my ponytail and blow around my face. I lifted my hand to push them back behind my ear when suddenly Gordie let out a yelp from his place beside me.

My shoe lost its footing and slid off the pedal, causing the handlebars to jerk to one side. I whipped my head around to see what the commotion was and, unfortunately, my body followed. The bike flew out from under me and I slammed into the gravel shoulder, my leg twisting beneath me.

Gordie started barking and darted out into the road. The approaching car swerved. The one that had been heading straight for us.

"Gordie!" I frantically called for him.

Behind me there was a whine and I thought for sure Gordie was plastered to the pavement. If I looked over to find him crushed beneath the car I would never forgive myself.

How much would Josh hate me now that I'd been responsible for killing his dog?

Cars were dangerous, whether you were inside one or not. I had been riding in the bike lane, the one specially paved and marked by the county to encourage green methods of transportation, and a car still managed to try and run me off the road.

Gordie had saved my life. He should have been at home with Josh, but I guess Gordie knew I needed him more than Josh did right now.

My heart was beating so fast that I had to put my hand over my chest to keep it from leaping out. I couldn't seem to get enough air even though I was breathing heavy like I'd just finished running a marathon.

When I tried to stand up, my knee screamed in protest. Just as I started to lift myself up on my hands in a push-up position, a warm tongue swiped across my cheek.

"Gordie!"

He smiled at me triumphantly, showing off a mouthful of jagged, crooked teeth. It was a beautiful sight.

"You're a good boy, Gordie. A good boy."

The driver of the car, panicked and gasping for breath, scrambled out of her car and rushed over. "Oh my god! I almost hit you! Are you all right?"

Her phone was gripped tight in her hand. She'd probably been texting and didn't see that she was about to run into me until Gordie jumped out in front of her to alert her.

I moved to a sitting position and inspected my knee. Pain sliced behind my kneecap, but nothing appeared to be broken. Thanks to Gordie, the car came a few inches from hitting me instead of head-on.

"I think my knee is messed up," I told her.

The pain in my knee was a welcome distraction from the pain in my heart.

My dad didn't say anything until the two of us we were alone in an exam room at the hospital. My knee had been wrapped up and determined as a sprain by a haggard young Emergency Room doctor and I was feeling stupid about falling off my bike.

"You weren't trying to…" Dad's question fell away as his eyes searched mine.

I shook my head. "It was just an accident, Dad," I assured him. "Some lady wasn't paying attention to where she was going and ran me off onto the shoulder."

Relieved that I wasn't suicidal, Dad nodded. I watched him swallow, his Adam's apple bobbing up and down beneath his beard. His big body took up most of the space inside the tiny room.

"I heard that you and Josh…had a falling out and I…thought the worst."

How had he heard about Josh and me? I hadn't told him. Boy, the grapevine in this town sure ran smoothly.

"Nothing morbid happened, Dad. Gordie showed up at the house and I was just making sure he got home okay."

Dad shoved his hands into his pockets and rocked back on his heels. Even though I was sitting up on the exam table, he still managed to loom over me. "I put Gordo in the truck. Warren's going to come by and get him."

Oh, so that's how Dad knew. Josh must have his told his father and Warren told Dad. Probably to make sure I wasn't let onto the property by mistake. How thoughtful of him.

I nodded and tried not to wonder if Josh would come with his father to pick up Gordie. Why would he? He wasn't under any obligation to make sure I was all right. He'd already made his feelings perfectly clear.

Movement in the doorway caught my eye and I looked up to see Josh in his wheelchair.

"Hey, Mr. Thornley," he said. "Carli."

"Josh!" Dad blurted out a little too excitedly.

"Josh," I murmured.

"My dad is in the parking lot," Josh addressed my dad. "Can you open your truck for him?"

"Sure. Yeah. I'll just leave you two kids alone." With the grace of a water buffalo, Dad maneuvered around Josh in his wheelchair and ambled down the hall.

"Your dad called me," Josh explained when we were alone.

I assumed he'd still be mad at me, but he looked at me like the other day never happened. I wished it could be wiped from my memory so easily.

Frowning, I looked down at his wheelchair. It must have taken some effort on Warren's part to get that thing into his trunk.

"I'm still too weak to stand for long periods of time," Josh explained unnecessarily.

"You'll get stronger," I assured him. He was already so much stronger than he had been. He might view his fatigue as a weakness, but I knew everything he'd been through. I knew he was as strong as an ox. I knew he was a warrior.

I quickly reminded myself that he didn't love me. Not the way I loved him. But my heart twisted inside my chest anyway. He was so amazing. He had the beauty of a boy and the strength of a man.

And I couldn't have him.

It felt strange sitting on a hospital bed with Josh looking up at me, a worried expression creasing his face. Would we ever have a relationship that didn't involve IV drips and beeping heart rate monitors again?

"It seems we've switched roles," Josh said, nodding toward the bed.

I almost said I preferred things the other way around, but seeing him laid up in a hospital again just might destroy what was left of me. Adversity was supposed to make you stronger, but my insides and outsides felt more fragile than ever.

"They're just keeping me for observation."

"You make it sound so creepy."

I bit down on my tongue to keep from cracking up. Josh could always find a way to make me laugh. Even when he'd been an idiot to me. "Is Gordie okay?"

"Why am I surprised?" he asked with a shake of his head. "You're always worried about everyone else. Yes, he's fine," he said when I shot him an unappreciative glare. "He's acting like nothing even happened."

Can't we do that, too? I wanted to ask. Can't we go back to how things were, when we were a part of each other's lives?

Josh stood up from the wheelchair and I put my hand out to stop him. "You don't have to get up."

Irritation flickered in his eyes. "Jeez, Carli, let me stand here in front of you like a man."

I clenched my jaw shut and ground my teeth together as I watched him wince and struggle to get to his feet.

"I would have walked in here, but the wheels were faster."

He'd rushed in to the hospital to see me.

"I didn't mean to worry you." I told him. "Especially after what happened—"

"Carli." His face had a hard edge to it, his eyes so intense that it felt like he could see right through me. He looked vulnerable and strong, all at the same time. "I love you."

When I opened my mouth to speak, he rushed on before I could get a word in. Before I could stop him from saying anything else he might regret. "I should have told you a long time ago, but I guess I took you for granted because you were always there for me. I've loved you for a long time, Carlina. And I was just too much of a coward to say it out loud."

I tried to blink back the tears, but it was too late. "Josh. You're the bravest person I know."

He shook his head and clasped my hand in his. "No," he whispered as he kissed my knuckles. "You are. Will you forgive me for being such a jerk to you?"

I took a few seconds and pretended to think about it. "I guess so," I answered cautiously.

This time he smacked me on the shoulder. "I'm sorry."

The second the words left his mouth I felt awful that he'd had the need to say them to me. "I'm sorry, too. I pushed you too hard and expected everything to suddenly go back to the way it was and—"

Too fatigued to argue, he put his hand up to stop me from rambling on about my guilt. "I shouldn't have yelled at you."

"I shouldn't have smothered you."

He tilted his head and gave me a look that said "Are you going to accept my apology or keep throwing it in my face?"

"I accept your apology. *If* you accept mine."

He nodded and put his arms out, gesturing for me to come in for a hug. He pulled me against his chest and I sighed. Even though it felt good, the hug confirmed how thin he was and I tried not to press too hard for fear of hurting him.

Come to think of it, this was the first time we'd hugged since he'd woken up—not counting the embrace during our kiss. It wasn't like we sat around hugging each other all day before the accident, but it was nice to have the physical connection with him after everything we'd been through.

Josh pulled away and looked into my eyes. "I'm sorry I was a jerk to you. It's just that ever since I woke up they've been poking and prodding at me. My mom is smothering me to death and she can't stop crying."

"I'm sorry I didn't give you enough space."

"Please. Don't be. I like it when you're around. You're my best friend and I want to be much more than that."

He reached out and touched my hand. I tried not to be startled by the fact that he had control of his movements again. For so long I'd sat and watched his unmoving form that I was still getting used to him being up and around. Well, up for the most part anyway. Despite depending on the wheelchair and the walker, he was doing a little more each and every day.

His brows came together as he studied the bandage on my knee. "I don't like seeing you bruised and scratched up." His voice was so tender that tears pricked the backs of my eyes.

"I had a lot of them after the accident." But he hadn't been awake to see them then.

"I'm sorry."

"What for?" He couldn't possibly have any more reasons to be sorry for anything.

"For not being there for you. Afterwards."

I closed my eyes tight and tried to shove away the memories of being all alone, watching his lifeless body for any sign of life. Having no one to talk to for months hadn't been the worst part. It was knowing that he might never wake up. That I might never hear him laugh again. Or see him smile at me.

Not wanting to miss a second of him being awake, I opened my eyes again and looked at him. "I'm just glad you're back."

"It was weird waking up this morning and not seeing you."

"I…you said you didn't want me around."

"And so you decided to play chicken with a car?"

"I *didn't*…" When I saw the look on his face and realized he was just trying to get a rise out of me, I clamped my mouth shut.

Man, it was good to have him back.

He looked at me wide-eyed and quickly smiled. And then he bent over to get something out of the pocket on the wheelchair. Tossing the journal onto the bed next to me, he commented, "I had no idea."

About which part? I asked myself. The part about how I had waited for him every day or the part about my hidden feelings for him? Well, I guess they weren't hidden any more. I had laid it all out for him, day by endless day.

"I read every word," he said, nodding toward the journal.

"So now you know everything."

"What you wrote down anyway."

We both knew I'd written down too much.

"And now I know that you love me back."

"Yeah." A red flush crept up his neck and he looked away. He raked shaky fingers through his hair.

It didn't take long for me to realize I had used up all the time he'd allotted for standing around talking about our feelings.

"Nice hat," I said, tipping the bill of the Razors hat he was wearing over his shaggy hair.

He met my gaze again, his green eyes sparkling. "You won it for me?"

"Yeah, I did." He'd read about it in the journal, so I knew I didn't have to tell him the details.

"Cody Lambert came to my house yesterday. That was your doing, right? I know my parents didn't set something like that up."

"Yeah." I had set it up. Despite Josh telling me to get a life that didn't involve him, I had set up a meeting for him with his idol. Because I didn't know how to not love him.

Josh was beaming. "He brought me a puck, and a jersey signed by the entire team. The *entire* team, Car. Do you know how freakin' *awesome* that is?"

"I want to see it."

"Sure." He had that crooked smile on his face. And it was good to see it make an appearance again after such a long hiatus.

"Soooo," I exaggerated, "how about getting us some hockey tickets? Now that you're all buddy-buddy with the *entire* team and all."

He flashed that grin at me again and suddenly my knee didn't hurt so badly anymore.

Two weeks later, my knee was all healed and I was back at Josh's house, hanging out with him until it was time for him to go to PT.

"My mom is going to rehab," Josh announced while he laced up his shoes.

I nodded. If he was trying to shock me with the news, he hadn't succeeded. It didn't take a genius to figure out that because Warren started spending more time at home, Catherine had a difficult time keeping her drinking problem under wraps.

Josh studied my face. "Things were rough around here this summer, weren't they?"

I tried to shrug off the last few months, but it wasn't an easy thing to do. "I'm glad she's finally getting some help."

"Me, too."

"She'll be fine."

There was a knock on the door. "Josh?" Catherine called from outside.

"What do you want, Mom?" Their relationship was strained and Josh was often short with her. At least he remembered who she was.

"You have five minutes to get ready for your physical therapy appointment," Catherine replied.

Josh grumbled under his breath. "Okay," he yelled at the door.

"I'll come back later," I said, standing up to leave. There were plenty of things to keep me busy at home. Like laundry and homework and studying for my upcoming AP Biology test.

"Stay here. You can use my computer for your homework."

"Are you sure?" I knew he needed his own space and I was willing to respect that. I was willing to do whatever it took to be in his life.

"Yeah." He stopped in his tracks and smiled at me.

He was inviting me back into his space and wild horses couldn't drag me away.

"Okay," I said with a smile.

"We can watch a movie when I get back." And then he was gone.

It was so nice to see Josh up and moving around. For so long it had been just a statue of him lying in his bed that I had to keep reminding myself that he was back.

He was back and he wanted me to stay.

When Josh got back from therapy, his face was ashen and his eyes bloodshot.

Catherine hovered around him.

"I got it, Mom!" he shouted at her.

"Let me at least help you into bed."

"No, Mom. I can do it myself."

I felt awkward sitting there watching Josh bicker with his mom.

He crawled into bed and let out a sigh. His whole body shuddered.

When his mom left and shut the door behind her, Josh sighed again. "That was brutal."

I packed my things into my backpack and stood up. "I'll let you get some rest."

"Carlina?"

"Yeah?"

"Don't go."

"I probably should, so you can get some sleep." Just because I worded it differently the second time didn't mean it would convince Josh.

"Come here." He reached his hand out and I went to him. He pulled back the covers and patted the empty space next to him.

Without a word, I climbed in next to him, careful not to bump him, and snuggled into his warmth.

The next sigh he released was one of contentment. He smoothed my hair away from my face and ran his thumb down my cheek. "I'm glad it was me and not you."

My chest tightened. "I'd be strong enough."

"Yeah, but I'd rather go through it than you."

He ran his fingers over the scar on my arm. "I'm glad nothing happened to you. I don't know what I would have done."

Fortunately, neither one of us would have to find out.

Chapter Twenty

Peach Pomatto was a force of nature, bathed in peach-scented body spray and draped in an orange ensemble of capri pants, a peasant blouse, and chunky orange-sorbet colored sandals. Her hair (orange, of course) was poofed and hairsprayed within an inch of its life, and would have made a Southern lady proud. She even *smelled* like peaches. Not only was she quite the fashion statement, she was the best hairdresser in all of Red Valley.

"I was so excited at the idea of making a housecall that I nearly tripped over my precious little Bean!" Peach exclaimed as she draped a cape over Josh's shoulders. With deft fingers, she started snipping away at Josh's shaggy hair.

Bean was Peach's Chihuahua. Apparently she brought him everywhere with her and he was currently perched on top of Josh's bed, looking like he owned the place.

By the look on his scraggly face, Gordie didn't know what to think of the intruder.

For the next half hour, I watched as Peach combed, shaved, cut, and transformed Josh back into the clean-cut boy I used to know.

"Next time I'll give you a nice deep conditioning treatment," she told Josh as she brushed the loose hair from his neck. "Your scalp is drier than the Sahara, sweetie."

"I didn't make time to moisturize," Josh replied deadpan. "You know, with being in the coma and all."

Peach tossed her head back and let out a delighted whoop. "Good thing all that sleeping didn't take away your sense of humor!"

By the time Peach loaded up her arsenal of hairstyling tools, we were all smiling. With a new haircut, Josh looked better than he had in months. He felt better, too. I could tell by the wide grin stretching across his face.

He wanted to look his best for his big public appearance the next day.

Josh Thornton stood in the middle of the August Lake High School gymnasium. The bleachers had been pulled out and hundreds of kids, Freshmen through Seniors, had their eyes glued to him. As expected, Josh didn't look the least bit nervous. In fact, he joked with the teachers and administrative staff as he took his place behind the podium. After adjusting the microphone, Josh began to speak.

His words were shaky and hesitant, but everyone wanted to hear what he had to say, badly enough to be patient as he slowly addressed the crowd. The assembly was in his honor and he was thrilled to tell everyone about his miraculous recovery.

"There was someone who stood by me the entire time during the coma and all throughout my recovery. I'm not talking about my mom or my dad or the doctors and nurses. I'm talking about my best friend, Carlina Thornley. She refused to give up on me. And because of her hope and her strength and her support, I didn't give up on myself."

Our eyes locked from across the crowded auditorium.

Thank you, he mouthed.

You're welcome, I mouthed back. And I smiled at him through a fresh batch of tears.

Later, Josh took questions from the audience, mostly kids asking what it was like being in a coma. Even though it was guaranteed to be taxing on his still fragile condition, he agreed. Because he didn't want people to make assumptions about him or listen to the gossip that swirled through campus on a daily basis. He wanted to inspire kids our age to never give up on themselves or their dreams, no matter the circumstances.

He adored being the center of attention once again and they had to practically rip the microphone out of his hands when it was over.

That was Josh. Always a sucker for the limelight.

Before we knew it, the seasons changed again and fall turned into winter and winter bloomed into spring again. The holidays had passed in a blur, but they were memorable because Josh made them that way. We were graduating from high school in a few weeks and I knew there was still a certain chapter in our lives we needed to shelve.

Now that Josh's recovery had progressed to the point where he could walk and stand on his own for longer periods of time, there was something he was ready to see.

I might have driven to our destination like an old lady, but I wasn't about to risk being blindsided by another idiot in an SUV. For the first few minutes of the drive we were both quiet, caught up in our own private thoughts.

Slowing down so that Josh could have a long look, I drove him by the corner house that had burned down last year. If you didn't know it had burned down you'd never know because the contractors had rebuilt the exact same house. They didn't even change the paint color.

"You waited long enough to get your license." Josh's comment broke the silence as I drove us out of town.

Without taking my eyes off the road I could tell that he was smirking. "I've had it since last August," I defended, flicking on my turn signal and easing into the turn lane.

"That's not what I meant."

"Then what did you mean, Mr. Backseat Driver?"

He looked pensively out the window. "Why didn't you get it while I was in the coma? That would've kept you busy for a while instead of hovering over me for months on end."

Not holding back, I smacked him in the shoulder—hard—and turned into the driveway of Gus Enterprises. Colorful flags proclaiming a "big blowout sale" flapped in the wind. Gus had been having that same "sale" for the past decade.

"Forgive me if I had an aversion to cars after all we went through together," I said, parking the Jeep. My dad's big rig hadn't made me nervous to ride in, probably because it would take a lot more than an errant SUV to crunch it to bits, but that day when Rhoda had forced me to get into her little tin can of a car and ride on the freeway to Red Valley had been a nerve-wracking ordeal.

Shrugging, Josh unbuckled his seat belt and pushed open the door. "You're tough," was all he said as he scanned the rows of junker cars, obviously looking for the Camaro.

"Almost as tough as you," I commented as I got out of the Jeep and followed him to the entrance.

Hand in hand we stood at the entrance of Gus's junkyard and looked up at the sign framed with exhaust pipes.

"The car's over that way," I said, pointing over to the north side of the lot.

In a move I wasn't expecting, Josh put his hands on my shoulders and turned me toward him. "What are you hiding from?" he asked, tapping the rim of my sunglasses.

"Nothing," I answered, wincing at the defensiveness in my tone.

He reached up and gently slid the sunglasses off my face. I couldn't help but let out a sigh. Every time he touched me was like the first time. That tingly anticipation of what was to follow zinged through my body.

"Are you sure you want to see it?" I asked. My feet shifted nervously and I looked down at the gravel. "Maybe this wasn't such a good idea. Maybe—"

"Sshh." He pressed his finger to my lips before I could say anything else. And then he moved his finger away and touched his lips to mine. He cupped a hand behind my neck and pulled me a little closer. And then he deepened the kiss.

After making me breathless, Josh pulled away, smiling. "Now, lead the way and quit being such a wuss."

"Yeah, we'd better go before Gus kicks us out for PDA."

Before we could take two steps forward, a gravelly voice called out to us. "Hey there! I was wondering when you'd stop by to see your old friend Gus."

Happy to see us, Gus talked to Josh for a while and I slipped away and went to stand in front of the Camaro. I couldn't hear what they were saying, but it really didn't matter.

The last time I'd been here to stare at the wreckage I'd felt like the loneliest person on the planet.

Several minutes later, I heard Josh come up behind me. He walked a lot slower than he used to, careful and measured, like he was afraid he might stumble and fall down if he strode at his previous breakneck speed. Neither one of us were in a hurry the way we used to be. Time was more precious to us now and we both took measures to savor it more.

Josh stood next to me and laced his fingers with mine. I looked at the mutilated car in front of me and felt his warm hand in mine, reassuring me that I wasn't alone anymore.

In that moment, I could see past the wreckage and into our future where we tossed our caps into the air at graduation. I could see us dancing at Blake's wedding. I could see myself going off to college, knowing that Josh would be all right without me, waiting for me when I was finished. It was all there for us, the future laid out before us, shiny and new.

I had a long road ahead of me before I could achieve my dreams of becoming a doctor. But, along with all the other things Josh and I had learned together, I knew that that road was paved with support, friendship, and love.

If we ever needed a reminder of the events that happened last year, we could always reread my journal. But, as I stood there with Josh, looking at our past, I preferred to keep my eyes on the future, unknown obstacles and all.

Josh looked over at me, a funny look on his face. "You would have loved me anyway, even if I could never walk again."

"Yes, I would have. And I do."

"How did I get so lucky?"

"You're not lucky," I argued. Partly for the fun of it and partly because he expected me to. "You're stubborn."

"I'm in love with you, Carlina."

"I know," I said with a smug smile. Josh had taught me that love was stronger than doubt. "I love you, too." I gave Josh's hand a gentle squeeze.

He squeezed back.

Epilogue

Josh's candid honesty and humor made him an effective motivational speaker and I encouraged him to make a full-time career out of it. People benefited from hearing his story and his love for life reawakened their waning ambitions. He took my advice and later visited schools all across the country, motivating kids of ages and sharing his message of hope.

Cody Lambert stayed true to his word and kept in touch with Josh all during his recovery and long afterward. He even pulled some strings and got Josh an internship with the Razors organization where Josh eventually became the Vice President of Public Relations and Fan Development at the Razors Foundation.

Doors opened for Josh, and he walked right through them with his head held high and his spirit renewed. The path he had envisioned for himself before the accident differed greatly from what he actually ended up doing. But that was okay. He worked hard to get where he was and he still played a variety of sports in his free time for fun. Competitive as always, he put his heart and soul into everything he did.

Not being able to pursue playing pro hockey had been a low blow. One he hadn't expected or prepared himself for. Josh used humor to help deal with his disappointments.

"There's a reason I wasn't cut out to be a hockey player," he joked with me one day. "I wouldn't want to join the Razors and be so good that I put CoLa out of a job."

He'd always walk with a slight limp and he'd probably never be able to make a fist with his left hand again, but it wasn't enough to hold him back. I gave him time and space to mourn his losses, but he bounced back quickly, surprising us all.

Limitations were presented to him, but Josh had a special way of proving everyone wrong. He lived for it, thrived on it. Any time he could make someone eat their words, Josh gladly stepped up to the plate.

His life might have been modified, but at least he'd been given a second chance to live that life.

Although it was a rough journey, Catherine overcame her addiction to alcohol and started a non-profit organization to help children who had been in or were currently in a coma. Josh's Hope provided financial assistance and connected loved ones and caregivers with counselors. Warren spent less time at work and more time with his wife, helping others. Philanthropy was fulfilling work and it strengthened the Thornton's relationship and their marriage. Warren and Catherine stayed together for better or for worse, becoming role models for their two sons.

As soon as he had an empty nest, my dad began taking longer runs and went back to chasing those white dotted lines. We never heard from Aunt Rhoda again. Dad never remarried, telling me that he'd had his one shot at love with my mom. He remained my biggest cheerleader and he cried—all four-hundred pounds of him—the day he walked me down the aisle and transferred my arm from his to Josh's.

I never took off the locket necklace Josh gave me, and I never stopped loving him through the good times and the bad. I decided to specialize in oncology and when I graduated from med school—with the snazzy new title of Dr. Carlina G. Thornton, MD—Josh was there waiting for me with a bouquet of red roses and that lopsided smile of his.

"You're here," I said, breathless from all the ceremony excitement around me. Agatha was there, too, along with my dad and Josh's parents, all crowded together taking photos and laughing and talking.

Josh took my hand in his and pulled me close for a kiss. With the flowers crushed between us, he pulled back and looked deep into my eyes. "I never left."

About the Author

Rachelle Vaughn is the author of the Razors Ice books, a series of hockey-themed romance novels. She lives in California with her husband and their sassy calico cat. When she isn't writing, Rachelle enjoys watching action movies, snapping photos for her birding blog, Wings and Daydreams, and cheering for her favorite hockey players.

Visit her website at rachellevaughn.com.

Score big with more heartwarming romance
from Amazon Bestselling Author
Rachelle Vaughn
Don't miss the bestselling Razors Ice series!

HOME ICE
FRESH ICE
WILD ICE
HOT ICE
BLIND ICE
ISLAND ICE

From the magical charm of a cottage in the wetlands…
to the heated passion of a mountain getaway…
these hot and sweet romances will have you falling in love
with hockey all over again!

Made in the USA
Middletown, DE
09 April 2022

63908307R00132